"Tell me, what is it that you plan to do
with your one wild and precious life?"

A Summer Day

Mary Oliver

# Chapter 1 - An Envelope

It was 4am on May Day in Oxford and Christ Church Meadow was lying in a dreamland of darkness and mist. The outline of the ancient university buildings was still visible beyond, their gothic spires and baroque domes illuminated by the moon. On the ground the streets were quiet, aside from occasional groups of students staggering home from university balls, laughing with shirts unbuttoned and dresses crinkled. And a single blackbird atop the tallest building, Magdalen Tower, cried out its sweet song as it caught the first glimmer of sun far away on the horizon.

A solitary cloaked figure on a bicycle swept under the Bridge of Sighs, then wound its way between the narrow walls of New College Lane. Professor Drake took this route at this exact time on this exact date every year. He called it the witching hour due to the unpredictability of its nature. He was tired and crotchety, having been up all night marking essays, and had already tumbled off his bike when a figure in a horned pagan mask leapt into his path.

"Watch where you're going you idiot!" he'd cried out shaking his fist, furious with the shrouded villain who'd dared to disrupt his ritual. Then he'd quietly cursed as he retrieved a worn-out leather satchel which had flown from his basket into the empty road.

It was extremely out of character for Andrew Drake to lose his temper. With his soft face, bespectacled blue eyes and unkept mousy hair, coiffed courtesy of his bicycle's airstream, he was known for his mild manners and easy going nature. He managed those who were meddlesome with warmth and good humour and offered others the goodwill he would hope for himself. But the first of May was a date of particular importance, on which Andrew could be forgiven for breaking his conduct, as he raced towards his destination ahead of the big rush.

He heard the familiar whirring and clicking of his brakes as he started to slow down on Queens Lane. Then he pulled up outside his college and locked up his bike. An incessant drizzle had plagued the city during the early hours and the air still felt heavy and dank.

"Why do I still put myself through this?" he grumbled, as he squeezed his bike between a row of tightly packed spokes, then fumbled with his lock in the dark. But he'd made it this far and there was little point or likelihood that he would turn back now.

He tugged the distressed strap of his satchel across his lithe body, bundled up in two woollen sweaters and a thermal vest, underneath his long black gown. Then he made his way towards the old cafe on the corner, turned left onto the High Street, and walked the short distance to Magdalen Bridge.

Despite Andrew's early start he was always astonished by how many people were ahead of him, huddled on blankets with hot drinks near the base of Magdalen Tower, in anticipation of the tens of thousands of others soon expected to flock there. He'd been taking this solemn pilgrimage for the past ten years, though his memories of May Day celebrations stretched back decades and were happy and hazy prior to this. Squeezing past strangers who were either sleep deprived, drunk, or both, he swore as he did every year, that this would be his last. As an erudite man whose intellect was honed behind the very walls in front of him, his rational mind warned his annual custom would unlikely bring the solace he so desperately craved. But as a romantic, who had loved gallantly and lost tragically, his heart was now hopelessly bound to the tradition. *They say bargaining is the third stage of grief* he thought, as he gazed at the wise-faced gargoyles staring back at him from the college's castle like battalions. Yet something deep inside still uttered that his commitment to this practice might one day offer a resolution.

Andrew wove between tuxedoed youths, swaying unsteadily with half empty bottles of champagne, and women in tight dresses whose faces looked unreasonably fresh despite smudges of last night's makeup beneath their eyes. Finding one of the last squares of space furthest away from Magdalen Tower, he glanced at the wooden punts lined up on the river below, before pulling a blanket and flask from his bag and hunkering himself down.

It was almost 4.30 and the darkness of the bridge was balmed in the amber glow of street lamps. Thrushes and robins were now out to join the blackbirds, piercing the air with their melodic chorus. Resting his head against the bridge's rigid stone, Andrew closed his eyes, and let their dawn cries salve him. Enclosed within his private universe, he sensed the presence of the human souls surrounding him, each with a unique story that led them to the exact same place as him. Each with their own hopes and dreams, memories of heavenly days gone by, never to be regained, and mortal fears for how few might remain. And just like him, many would understand how it feels to love so ferociously that, in amongst the endless summer days languishing in the wonder of another being, and candlelight evenings where the meaning of life is revealed in your lover's eyes, lies a fear: a deep and wretched knowing that one day it will all end. Until finally it does.

Just as Andrew was drifting to that moment when the self becomes nebulous before sleep, a prodding in his shoulder brought him back to earth with a bump. Feeling even more violated than he had by his masked assailant, he snapped his eyes open to an unthreatening assortment of bells and brightly coloured ribbons. He slowly raised his head past the three quarter length trousers attached, until it landed on a gentleman's face. It was fulsome and jolly with eyes full of hope with a nose pink as rhubarb from the morning chill. His soft top hat was adorned with summer flowers, above hair as white as a West Highland terrier. Andrew braced as he opened his mouth to speak:

"Oh I do beg your pardon," said the man with affected politeness in a musical Black Country accent.

"I wasn't meaning to disturb you or anything. It's just I'm here for the Maypole dancing later you see," he said gesturing to a generous belly, buttoned tight over a yellow waistcoat.

"Could do with taking the weight off for a minute or two. Or else me poor old trotters will be fit for nothing by the time it comes to me big moment."

He tapped a pair of surprisingly dainty black shoes together, making his bells do an explanatory jingle. Andrew inwardly groaned at the unwanted disturbance. His body was aching and sore from his fall, with nerves that were starting to ease, now piqued and agitated. But seeing the longing in the benevolent face above him, and tickled by its incongruous attire, he said:

"Of course. Take a seat," in his soft Yorkshire accent, to the man jingling again as he shuffled his way down, leaving him little time to make space. He slumped against the wall, which made his hat fall below his eyes and let out an exaggerated sigh of relief. Then he lifted the back of his hat, flipped it over his head revealing large pink ears, then bowled it down his arm into his lap. Hopeful of an acknowledgment of his nifty party trick he instantly turned to Andrew. Then spotting his black gown, he broke into a smile that made his whole face appear to expand.

"Well well well. Some sort of teacher are you then? Work at the university do you?" he asked, eyes wide with admiration. Andrew had got used to the attention his gown received from people who weren't from the city, having been asked by tourists more times than he could remember to stop and have his photograph taken. But remembering his own mix of curiosity and amazement when he first arrived as a wide eyed eighteen year old, it never bothered him.

"I do," he replied politely.

"I'm a professor here actually."

"Well I'll be blown," said the gentleman, lifting his furry white eyebrows in awe.

"Here's me, first time in Oxford, and I'm already jabbering away at a genius."

Andrew shook his head modestly to play down the compliment, but without noticing the man steamed on.

"Course I never went to college or the like. In my day you went to school until you did your O levels, and that was that. Did my electrician's apprenticeship down the coal mine when I was fifteen, then it was eight years' hard graft underground until I'd made enough money to start up on my own."

Then a look of horror shot across the man's face, which caused his cheeks to turn the same shade of rhubarb to his nose. He rubbed a large hand vigorously on his trousers before extending it out with another jingle.

"Oh where are my manners? I'm Bernard by the way. I've come all the way from Birmingham, you know," he added, as if his accent hadn't already given this away.

"I only took up Morris Dancing cos my mate Mervin down the Horn and Trumpet said they all go for a beer after. And look at me now. I'll be dancing around the maypole in Radcliffe Square later. You could come and watch if you liked?"

Andrew, starting to warm to this jovial character, whose unfiltered chat revealed genuine warmth and who had already helped him kill some time, took his hand and gave it a firm shake.

"And I'm Professor Drake, but you can call me Andrew. It's very nice to meet you Bernard. I will try my best to take you up on that very fine offer."

The pair chattered away, watching the crowds of bleary eyed students and flower-strewn bohemians, packed from the bridge down the length of the High Street. Andrew had always been more of a listener than a talker, which came in handy when students were nestled before a fire in his oak beamed study reading essays aloud, drowsy from writing through the night. He loved hearing other people's stories: each of them a unique tale full of vibrant characters, whose own narratives shaped them into the multifaceted human they are today. With gloved fingers wrapped around his coffee cup, he watched darkness slowly succumb to morning light with Bernard's animated storytelling as an accompanying soundtrack. He learned of his humble origins as the son of a stern but hard working Midlands coal miner and pictured an earnest, well intentioned boy, with a thick head of chestnut hair and protruding ears that added to his endearing character. He imagined him kneeling by a tin bath, red kneed, in short trousers and a woolly jumper, diligently scrubbing his father's back when he came home thick in coal dust. Then he saw the tears in his trusting eyes as he stood by his beloved mother's deathbed in a suit far too large for his gangly teenage frame. A voluptuous woman with a shiny black bouffant, red lipstick and a fur stole, sprung to mind when he described his mother's friend who rapidly married his widowed father. He felt the weight of his regret over a subsequent rift that hadn't healed by the time he turned up to his Dad's funeral like a virtual stranger. Then applauded his carpe diem attitude when describing how that led to him proposing to his beautiful wife Muriel, which resulted in the happy family he was so proud of today. It created the perfect arc of a classic story, in which Bernard was a particularly lovable and deserving hero in Andrew's humble opinion. Sitting in the crisp morning light, being warmed by his eagerness to share his tale, he was pleased that their paths had crossed. He wondered what difference this short encounter may have made to his own life, whose gentle ripples might make waves further down the road. Just as he was musing on the mystery of life: with its chaos and order, cause and effects, each of us a tiny butterfly directing the cosmic plot, the clock tower struck six and the crowd, and even Bernard, fell silent.

Andrew's face instantly became solemn and he rose to his feet, followed by a bashful Bernard who was trying his best not to jingle. No matter how many times he stood in this spot it would always take him back to the moment that had shaped his life, in ways he hadn't even known were possible. Then he lifted his head, gazing almost one hundred and fifty feet up to the top of the tower.

The sky was awakening with morning light with the sun rising up from the ground to meet it. The roof of Magdalen College was smouldering with ethereal sunbeams as they climbed atop its ancient walls. It was a sight that could inspire hope and joy in the hardest of hearts. But since Andrew's had been lost a long time ago, all he could do was watch and wait. Out of nowhere the sky erupted with a sound which might have been straight from the heavens: a hauntingly beautiful hymn, sung in Latin by voices as pure as angels.

Andrew remained sombre with his hands by his side, eyes fixed, almost unnervingly, on the top of the tower. Bernard looked from the turret to Andrew in turn, his mouth wide with wonder. He wondered what his new friend might be thinking, and could have sworn he saw his eyes fill with tears. He'd been so busy talking about himself: how he lived in a part of Solihull where house prices were going up, had three grown up children and that when he wasn't Morris Dancing he enjoyed garden bowls, playing the French horn and holidaying with Muriel in their caravan in Wales, that he hadn't asked Andrew much about himself. Earlier in the morning he'd tiptoed between hundreds of people crouched on the bridge not daring to ask for space. But something about this gentle faced man sitting alone, who couldn't be older than his mid forties, had made him think he might be open to his company.

Sensing the younger man also had a story, he now wondered if he had a spouse or any children. Muriel would always gently reign him in when he got carried away sharing his anecdotes. But he was having such a lovely time with Andrew, who was such a good listener, time had flown before he'd had a chance to ask him any questions.

"You big numpty Bernard," he silently scolded, patting his belly sheepishly and regretting that terribly now. He gazed up at the tower again, wondering how those singers must be feeling: so high in the sky, doing something they loved and had practised to perfection, just like him and his Morris Dancing. As the choir silenced he heard the bells ring out brightly as they would for the next twenty minutes. Andrew took off his spectacles and gave them a quick rub on his cloak, before turning to Bernard and asking:

"So what did you think?"

For the first time since they'd met, Bernard was totally speechless. He blinked at Andrew for sometime before gathering himself and saying:

"It was… magnificent!"

He pronounced the word with such heartfelt passion it made Andrew feel a little overcome.

"And they do that every year do they?"

"Yep," said Andrew.

"Every year for the last five hundred or so. Goes right back to Henry VIII's day. It's called the Hymnus Eucharisticus, sang to music by a former student to welcome the rising sun and the start of Summer:

'We worship you, O God the Father, we offer you our praise, for you nourish our bodies, and minds with heavenly grace'."

After Andrew had recited the opening lines of the hymn, Bernard was rendered speechless once again. He stared at him, with his eyes glistening, before repeating:

"Well I'll be blown."

"Well it was a real pleasure meeting you Bernard," said Andrew, holding out his hand, which Bernard grabbed, before pulling him in and patting his back in a vigorous jingling hug. Then, with a jolt of sadness that their special moment had come to an end Bernard hesitantly asked:

"And do you think you might be able to come and watch me dancing?" with a hopeful nod.

"I wouldn't miss it," Andrew replied warmly.

Then, breaking into a grin which made his face puff up like a pink balloon, Bernard docked his top hat with a delighted "Toodle Oo" then vanished into the departing crowds.

As soon as Bernard was out of sight, and with the crowds rapidly dispersing, Andrew reached into his satchel. Turning to the bridge he drew out a single white rose, and placed it tenderly to his lips, before dropping it and watching it float down river. Then he joined the rest of the throngs meandering back towards the city for early breakfasts and hair of the dog drinks.

He turned back onto Queen's Lane, then right, through the stone archway to St Edmund Hall, or "Teddy Hall" as it was more affectionately known.

"Morning Mr Frogmore," he said brightly to the college porter, as he passed his window on his way through the lodge.

"Is it?" he grumbled, without lowering his newspaper or

bothering to see who was there.

Andrew felt a welcome sense of homeliness as he entered the pretty front quad which was already busy with people milling around celebrating the start of May Day. Having studied at one of the larger colleges, the more compact and down to earth nature of Teddy Hall had appealed once he became a professor. It had a perfect rectangular lawn, surrounded by a path and four walls of quaint, old buildings with a soft golden hew. The most striking building stood across the lawn and was once an Archbishop of Canterbury's house, way back in the thirteenth century. Now it was a long rustic dwelling with dainty pointed garrets and leaded windows nestled in mediaeval stone. There was a large blue sundial just below the roof and rambling roses and wisteria hanging off its walls. A small but handsome chapel stood at the end of the quad, with grand entrance pillars running from the ground right up to the roof. And they all overlooked an ancient stone well which looked enchanting in the middle of the lawn.

Andrew was making his way towards his study, picturing himself collapsing into its huge sofa, when a small caped figure blocked his path.

"Ahhh Professor Drake!"

A man had appeared in a cap and gown which swished into the air like a dragon's tail when he leapt from a doorway. Mr Bartholomew, the college dean, was as notorious for his unexpected arrivals as his ability to pry into other people's business. He had a sallow pinched face with a tight mouth which generally looked poised to incriminate.

"I'm so glad to have caught you bright and early this morning. Although I'm fully aware that you never miss the May Day choir," he went on, eyeing Andrew suspiciously through dark oval spectacles, which gave him a villainous air.

*And I'm fully aware that you never miss anything*, is how Andrew wanted to reply. But he smiled graciously and said:

"It's a wonderful tradition," as politely as he could bear.

"And will you be joining us for formal hall this Sunday, Professor?" Mr Barthomew went on, in a voice brusque enough to bite.

"We haven't seen you at the top table in quite some time."

Andrew was aware the word "we" was applied to add weight to his accusation, yet he still felt a sting of embarrassment. Although most of Oxford's quirks and traditions appealed to him, formal dining in gowns was far from top of his list. He found the etiquette overly stuffy and the small talk far too stifling. But, caught in the Dean's dead eyed stare, he nodded and said.

"Of course Sir. Looking forward to it."

"Splendid!" Mr Bartholomew exclaimed, squeezing his fingertips together like a church steeple.

"We'll look forward to seeing you then. Good day to you Professor," he added, with an unnecessary sweep of his cloak, before making his way off down the path.

*Good day to you Professor*! Andrew rolled his eyes and chuckled to himself, certain even Mr Bartholomew must know his decorative speech sounded ridiculous in this day and age.

"Oh and one more thing Professor..."

Mr Bartholomew had turned the corner and was about to fire his parting shot across the lawn.

"Don't forget that guests *are* welcome!" he announced with glee, making several sleepy students spin around. Then he swished and disappeared into another doorway, just as quickly as he'd appeared.

Andrew felt his jaw tighten as he carried on down the path, past the old dining room, which he'd been summoned to whether he liked it or not. It was a beautiful space, he had to admit, with its tall leaded windows with their pretty stone arches, offering a glimpse of fine oil paintings within. Plus its diminutive size meant it wasn't intimidating like the more stately halls he acknowledged, turning past the college bar with colourful rowing oars hanging from the ceiling. But it was that very intimacy that bothered him, he confessed as he headed through an open doorway and began stomping up a spiral stone staircase towards his study. One of the things he liked less about this little college was the fact it made it difficult to keep one's private life exactly that: *private*. With his key in his hand, he heard the tired old creak of a wooden door, confirming he'd finally made it back to his sanctuary.

He plonked his satchel on a mahogany coffee table in the centre of the room, then let out a wheeze, as his bones sunk into the soft cream sofa beneath him. Shutting his eyes, he took a slow deep breath in and out. He'd done it.

He could hear the steady, recurrent phrases of a song thrush drifting through his window and breathed in the familiar musty smell of ancient floorboards beneath a well worn Persian rug. Nestled in his cocoon of beloved bookcases, away from the morning crowds and prying eyes, every fibre of his body longed to light the fire, grab a blanket and fall into a deep, deep slumber right there for the rest of the day. It had been a long night, and an even longer morning with its many disturbances. He could feel his eyelids getting heavier, with faint images beginning to flicker in front of his eyes: a sinister mask with twisted horns; silver bells and coloured ribbons; morning sun flickering through leaves; a mediaeval tower growing higher and higher; *a sudden flash of beautiful auburn hair*! Andrew's body jerked upright with his eyes wide open and his heart thumping against his chest. As his consciousness slowly calibrated, bringing him back into the present moment, he felt an odd mix of relief tinged with regret.

"For God's sake Drew, get a grip," he muttered, running his trembling fingers through his hair. Then he took a deep breath with his hands on his knees, before quietly locking up his study and retracing his steps back to the porter's lodge.

Mr Frogmore the college porter was a stout man in a bowler hat and suit, who liked to grumble in his thick south London accent. He was leaning back in his leather chair in his usual spot at the window overlooking the walkway into Teddy Hall. Having also been awake throughout the night, watching the comings and goings of students in various stages of inebriation, he appeared not to be in the best of spirits.

"Lovely morning this morning Mr Frogmore," said Andrew, walking up steps to a narrow room with wooden pigeon holes lining the wall.

"Well I'd like to know what's so lovely about it," said Mr Frogmore in his drawn out cockney drawl.

"Been run off my feet all night I have with drunken louts bothering me with silly questions: 'Where's this, where's that?' And the noise! Couldn't hear myself think. If it wasn't music booming it was fireworks banging, almost giving me a heart attack. Why anyone would want to stay up all night galavanting is a complete mystery to me. But then so much of what people get up to around here is a mystery to me."

Looking suspiciously over his glasses at Andrew, who was nonchalantly leafing through his post and stifling a yawn, he added:

"I take it you haven't been out dancing the night away Professor?"

"Certainly not Mr Frogmore," replied Andrew abruptly, appalled by the very suggestion.

"It was a somewhat wearing night though I must confess. I was up late marking essays, then swung by Magdalen this morning for old times sake. Looking forward to getting back home for a spot of much needed breakfast now."

"Still living on that house boat are we Professor? Oooh I happen it must get a bit chilly down there. Never seen the appeal of being around water myself. But then who am I to know what appeals to people these days."

"Yes, the barge. I'm still there Mr Frogmore. Suits me just fine for now," said Andrew guardedly, well aware that his unconventional living arrangements raised the eyebrows of many around the college.

"Better get a move on, come to mention it. Have a good day Mr Frogmore."

"I'll try my best Professor," he shot back gloomily, as Andrew made his way out of the lodge, towards his bike.

Still holding his post he glanced back down at it. There were three regular looking letters addressed to him. But the fourth had caught his attention. It was a small cream envelope with a red wax seal and one name written across the front in distinctive green letters: *Esmeralda*.

He paused briefly to look at it again, before putting his mail in his satchel and unlocking his bike.Then securing his bag firmly into the basket, lest he take another tumble, he swung on leg over his bicycle and began the journey back home.

# Chapter 2 - A Tea Party

It was the afternoon before May Day and a sky as blue as a cornflower was shot with thin beams of sun and soft wisps of clouds. Far below, in a village nestled in the Oxfordshire countryside, a beautiful riverside garden was being set for a very special tea party. A young woman in a long lemon dress, with ample puffed sleeves, was busily overseeing procedures. She had thick blonde hair chopped just below her shoulders which framed a pleasantly symmetrical face. Her eyes were as blue as the heavens above and her smile could light up a ballroom when she was satisfied with her circumstances. But right now it was set in a serious pout, which twisted from one side to the other, as she wrinkled her brow and flustered over details.

At just fifteen, Summer Hayes was more used to hosting parties than most people her age. Her family's home, Riverside Cottage, was an elegant white five bedroom house set in landscaped grounds on the riverbank. It had witnessed dozens of extravagant social events during its forty odd years as the family home. With its charming glass orangery with ornate spires, French doors leading to a soft stone patio, and steps winding to a garden which gently tumbled to the river, it had played host to many a champagne reception and marqueed ball. But today's event was to be Summer's closest friend's sixteenth birthday celebration and she was determined to make it perfect.

She'd been busy setting the scene since midday, under the shade of a straw boater, wrapped in a chiffon scarf which flowed gently down her back. A long wooden table, covered in a lace tablecloth, had been placed in a position she'd declared "suitably dreamy" beneath a weeping willow tree which floated partly into the river. Four wooden thrones, sprayed gold for her cousin Otto's winter wedding, were placed around it. She'd gathered dusk pink peonies from the garden and arranged them in one of her mother's finest cut glass vases as an "elegant but not too showy" centrepiece. Then she'd circled it with stands, tiered with china plates finely painted with graceful birds and golden trees.

"Hmm yes, I think it's getting there, getting there," she muttered studiously under her breath, taking the briefest of pauses to inspect her work. With a brain prone to hopscotching around topics and a mouth eager to keep up, concentration wasn't always Summer's strong point. But when it came to entertaining, or doing something special for those she loved, her mind would become as focussed as a research analyst. She was just about to start placing silver rings around linen napkins, when the wobble of a rickety ladder made her spin around.

"Be careful up that tree Daddy!" she cried out to Harold Hayes: a heavy set former Navy Admiral in his early seventies, who'd been nimbly hanging a string of pompoms in pink, white and gold between two birch trees higher up the garden. As the willing ringmaster of most of the family's events, he was already dressed in a blazer the colour of his favourite Cabernet Sauvignon over a mustard waistcoat which matched his pocket handkerchief. He had thick grey hair, parted to one side, and a neatly combed moustache which wriggled when he talked.

"Aye aye captain," he shouted back, saluting to his daughter, never passing up an easy opportunity to overuse his naval terminology.

"*Both* hands back on the ladder please Daddy. *Now!*" Summer ordered, before swiftly adding:

"Right, it looks perfect, now please come down immediately before you break your neck."

Harold made his way precariously down the ladder, which

looked far too fragile to take his weight, before standing up stock straight and admiring his handy work. Reassured and mumbling "I'm actually rather chuffed with those bobbles," he did a little skip, bellowed a hearty "Right, back to the barracks," before marching under the pompoms and back to the house.

Just as Summer was about to refocus her scatterbrain on the task of artfully crafting her table settings, a sweet and refined woman's voice disrupted her flow again:

"Summer darling. I managed to find the rest of the decorations we used for Mummy's birthday shoved behind the ping pong table at the back of the garage, would you believe? I don't know how many times I have to tell your father that we store *'party items in the attic and sports gear in the garage'*. Anyway, where would you like them dear?"

Summer's mother Hyacinth Hayes, who was almost twenty years Harold's junior, was standing on the patio holding a square cardboard box, with 'Party Decorations KEEP DRY!' written in large red letters. She was slim and attractive with a sleek grey bob with a hint of lilac, and a subtle scent of lavender talcum powder followed wherever she went. A single strand of pearls adorned most of her outfits, which generally involved a touch of broderie anglaise and a stylish cigarette pant.

"Thanks Mummy. Just drop them at the bottom of the steps. Bambi's in charge of garden decorations. I'll get her to hang them from the trees when she arrives," Summer hollered back up the garden, before hurriedly getting back to her labour of love.

As if on cue, a loud doorbell belted out the rousing first bars of Vivaldi's Spring from the Four Seasons, followed by Harold's even louder voice saying:

"Bambi's here, I'll get it!"

The clomping of shoes on a polished wood floor was followed by a creaking door and a distant:

"Bambi darling, welcome aboard. They're just at the end of the garden. You know where to go. But brace yourself. My girl is running a particularly tight ship today!"

Then the sound of Harold chuckling to himself. Moments later Priya Bhambri, nicknamed Bambi by Summer, who had a pet name for everyone she adored, walked through the French doors onto the patio. She had big doe eyes and long slim legs, which, along with her rhyming surname, had earned her the name Bambi. An olive silk gown clung to her cocoa skin while a thick band of wildflowers crowned her long raven hair. She wore a smooth jade teardrop which hung almost to her navel and was carrying a large brass gong with a soft long hammer.

"Bambs. You look Ahh-mazing," shouted an excited Summer, taking a micro break from tittivating the table to glance up and admire her friend.

"Oh and thank you *so* much for bringing the things. Right. Just pop those down there for now. Mum's left some pompoms and other bits and bobs for the trees at the bottom of the steps."

By now Summer was fluttering rose petals from a wicker basket down the centre of the table, with a level of flamboyant artistic flourish worthy of a modern master.

"Hey no probs," said Priya, in her soft Scottish lilt, walking down the steps, with the steadiness of a figure skater compared to Summer's exuberant trampolinist. Priya Bhambri was the most effortlessly cool girl at Elm Tree Academy, thanks to her love of yoga and all things spiritual. Her sensible head had proven the perfect antidote to Summer's unpredictable exploits over the years. Summer had idolised Priya ever since she had moved to Oxford from the Highlands, with her parents and older brothers Kush and Kyan, when she was six years old. Her adoration was sealed when the new girl inexplicably took the blame after an art lesson got out of hand and Summer somehow turned the school's fountain pink.

Priya cherished her friendships and delighted in Summer's quirks, particularly the extravagant lengths she was willing to go to to make others happy. Gliding down the garden barefoot, with a silver toe ring and a tiny nose stud, she smiled at the latest of her friend's sumptuous and thoughtful offerings.

"You've done it again Miss Hayes," she declared in her warm tone, walking up behind Summer and giving her shoulders a tight squeeze.

"And you managed to find peonies. Perfect. She's going to love those. You know how much she adores flowers and their meanings."

"Peonies for female empowerment," Summer replied proudly, busily piling tiny sandwiches prepared by Hyacinth onto the stands.

"Great shout Bambs. Right if you wouldn't mind grabbing some of those decorations and sticking them around that would be great. She could be here any minute."

Summer took a second to step back and admire her flourishing table.

"Oooh it's starting to look great," she squeaked, her trademark smile starting to replace her twisty pout. Then quickly switching back to flustered and agitated, she yelled:

"Daisy. Pack it in. Leave Charles alone or your outfit it going to be ruined!"

Summer's five year old sister Daisy had insisted on being invited to the tea party once she heard there would be dressing up and cake. However, now in her pink ballet leotard and wrap-over chiffon skirt, with a string of daisies at a wonky angle on her head, she had already broken her side of the bargain which was to: *Be good.*

She was racing the family's energetic golden retriever Charles through the garden's water sprinklers and it was hard to discern who was having the most fun. If Charles' loud barking and ability to hoodwink the little girl by jumping one way then running the other was anything to go by, it would seem the dog had the edge.

"I said pack it in!" Summer went on to her sister, who was now giggling so hysterically it seemed inevitable an accident of some sort was imminent.

"Right. Come here at once. I need to tell you what your job is."

A reluctant Daisy sauntered sulkily over, dragging her feet and wiping wet hair which had stuck to her forehead away with a sticky hand.

"Now you remember whose birthday it is today don't you Dais?" Summer said, kneeling down next to her sister.

"Yesth Aunty Esthme," said the little girl, revealing two missing front teeth and the sweetest of lisps.

"And there's going to be cake."

"Yes that's right,"

"Now, you see this basket," Summer went on, handing her the one she'd been scattering petals down the table from.

"When Aunty Esme walks underneath that string of pom poms up there, what are you going to do?"

"Have sthome birthday cake," said the little girl, revealing her toothless grin again.

"Nooo. That's not quite what we agreed, is it Daisy? When Aunty Esme walks under the pompoms and we shout Happy Birthday you're going to grab handfuls of petals and throw them at her like confetti aren't you Daisy?"

"And *then* I can have cake," said the little girl defiantly, breaking into more hysterical giggles.

To which Summer simply said "I give up."

Then ran off towards the house shouting, "Mummy how are the macaroons coming along?"

Thirty minutes later, the scene was finally starting to take shape. The cake stands were full of cheese and cucumber and egg and cress sandwiches cut into perfect triangles; macaroons in pink, white and gold; scones with jam and clotted cream; and fresh strawberries and scotch quails eggs. Priya had decorated the trees and scattered crystals on top of the rose petals on the table. Her brass gong was standing proudly under the willow tree. The sound of a piano playing Tchaikovsky was now drifting from the fingers of the oldest Hayes sister Honeysuckle. It wafted through the French doors, and across the garden which was now baked in sunshine, and even Summer was starting to feel relaxed. Until the door bell's rendition of Vivaldi made everyone jump out of their skin and shout: "She's here!!!" sending Summer almost into complete delirium.

"I'll get it!" bellowed Harold, while Hyacinth trotted back through the French doors as fast as she could, after delivering a freshly brewed pot of tea to the table.

Summer was now hissing:

"Daisy grab the basket. Grab. The. Basket!"

While Priya was standing looking cooler than the cucumber sandwiches next to the gong. Then they heard chatter and laughter coming from the hallway, until Harold and their VIP guest finally appeared on the patio. Looking like a proud father at a wedding and holding her hand as if presenting a debutante at a ball, Harold started slowly walking her down the steps:

"Here she is the birthday girl," he announced, his voice still military but with a singly songy edge.

"And my goodness doesn't she look a picture?"

Esme Drake was walking barefoot down the steps wearing a long, white dress. It was made of feather light cotton covered in chiffon, wrapped across her body in a V. It hung loosely off her shoulders leaving her slender arms bare and was pulled tight around her waist with golden ribbons. As she stepped onto the garden, the fabrics caught on the breeze then drifted behind her like threads of gossamer.

"Look at her. She's like an angel sent from heaven," Summer said dreamily, placing her hand theatrically to her chest, spellbound by her friend's ethereal entrance.

Esme was a sensitive girl whose intelligence was vibrantly enriched by a colourful imagination. Her head was happiest in a book or behind an easel and her spirit soared in the beauty of the earth and stars. She had rich auburn hair smoothed back with three gold bands, which flowed over her shoulders as she floated down the garden. Her sparkling eyes of emerald green, were growing wide with amazement as she drew closer to the halcyon scene ahead of her. As she walked under the string of pom poms, lightly blowing in the breeze, the girls shouted "Happy Birthday!" in unison.

Hearing her cue Daisy flung her petals into the air, her outstretched hand turned up like a little star, getting more on her own head than on Esme. Job done, she flumped down on the floor cross legged and put the upturned basket on her head.

Esme laughed in delight at the scene around her, which made the freckles on her turned up nose crinkle, and the sunbeams in her eyes twinkle.

"I can't believe you've thrown me a tea party!" she cried, clapping her hands together in gratitude. Summer's face broke into an exhilarated grin. Then she clasped Esme to her, with a squeak of excitement, and said:

"Well what else? It's always time for tea at Riverbank Cottage!"

Kicking off her shoes, so she was barefoot like the other girls, Summer took a long step back. She slowly looked Esme up and down, then broke into another gratified smile:

"I cant believe our baby girl is all grown up. The first of us to reach her sweet sixteen. And your outfit is simply perfection."

Summer had sent out invites six weeks before and been meticulously planning the day ever since. They were printed in gold text on cream parchment paper with a golden border. They read:

Occasion: Esme's 16th birthday

Location: Riverbank cottage

Time: 4pm

Dresscode: Goddesses of the Forest

The other girls had grown accustomed to Summer's meticulous party planning, ever since she'd dressed her portly Shetland pony Valerie as a unicorn then dragged her into the house on her eleventh birthday. She'd filled the orangery with cherry blossom trees and ordered her friends to dress as fairytale princesses. All was going blissfully until Charles, who was a playful puppy full of untamed energy, startled poor Valerie, causing her to rear up and put her hoof through the castle-shaped birthday cake.

Back at the goddess party, Esme was explaining how she'd found the dress in a charity shop in Thame and stitched the gold ribbons on herself while her Dad made the headdress, when an impassioned Summer grabbed her hand:

"With your long white gown and russet locks you are Aphrodite. Goddess of beauty, pleasure and love, bringing harmony and joy to all who encounter her," she cried passionately, delighting in the dramatics of the scene. Then gesturing to Priya, who was tapping the gong's hammer nonchalantly against her leg beneath the tree, she went on:

"And then we have Gaia, the primordial Earth mother. Goddess of nature and fertility. Born at the dawn of creation and our great oracle."

Thrusting her hand in the air, as if brandishing a spear, she added:

"And I am Diana. Goddess of the hunt, the wilderness and the moon. Protector of feminine strength, as powerful as she is benevolent."

Then walking towards Daisy, who was already sitting at the table, reaching for the macaroons, she said:

"And finally we have our little Eros, who really should eat sandwiches and drink tea before helping herself to sweets," before smacking her hand, which made Daisy stick her tongue out, then dive straight back into the macaroons. Summer pulled out the throne facing the river, ushering a slightly overwhelmed Esme to sit, before seating herself opposite, looking enraptured with the proceedings so far. Priya, knowing it was her turn to lead the ceremony, started addressing the table in a deep, mellow voice:

"Now I want everyone to just close their eyes and take a deep breath in and out."

As the three girls started to relax and obey her instructions, she gently hit the brass gong, which echoed and reverberated.

"Just let the sounds wash over you," she went on, her voice melodic and soothing.

"Keep breathing in and out."

Esme could hear the sound of the river running by and the breeze rustling through the trees. Her jasmine skin was glowing with happiness as her body started to ease. She loved Summer's well intentioned enthusiasm but was always grateful to Priya for settling things down. Catching the smell of burning she surreptitiously opened one eye, to see Priya lighting a clump of sage.

"I want you to just keep breathing in and out while I cleanse the table, and banish any bad energy."

Priya started gliding around the table, like Mother Earth herself beneath her halo of vibrant blooms. She paused to waft the sage around each of her friends' bodies in turn, which made Summer let out a sigh of bliss and Daisy let out three loud sneezes. Then she swept it up and down the length of the table a few times before returning to the tree and softly banging the gong.

"And now just relax, and open your eyes."

The other girls slowly brought themselves back into the garden, blinking into the sunshine and smiling softly with contentment.

Then Summer leapt to her feet, beamed down at her perfect table and announced:

"And now it's time for tea!"

## Chapter 3 - A Lifetime of Adventures

With the tea party in full swing, and the plate stands' contents thoroughly decimated, Esme sat back and drank in the heartwarming scene. Daisy, knocked out from her garden capers plus too much sugar, was fast asleep and happily snoring to her left. While Summer was chatting ten to the dozen to Priya, who was batting her long lashes listening intently on the other side. Framed by blossoming trees, bright rays of sun and the occasional river boat drifting by, Esme imagined taking out her easel and paints and capturing the moment forever more. What a perfect day this had been.

It had started around 8am when her father had woken her in her little room on the barge with tea and pancakes in bed. He'd made them just the way she liked them: thick with chopped strawberries smothered in maple syrup and a fine sprinkle of icing sugar. Then he'd brought in a bunch of pink roses and a small box, wrapped up in silver paper with a fine ribbon tied in a bow. Inside was an antique gold watch, engraved on the back with the words:

"To my darling Esme, Love always, Dad."

His use of the word "always" had warmed her soul. Having brought her up on his own since she was small, she always noticed his subtle reassurances that he would never leave her. Looking down at it, gleaming on her wrist in the early evening sun, she thought how curious it was that it should represent both an object of time and timelessness to her. Esme was the type of girl who lived and loved so fervently, that she never wanted life's precious moments to end. She pictured them like tiny clouds, drifting through an infinite sky, never to be matched or mirrored again. And even if she caught one, to hold forever in her heart, the canvas of her mind would slowly fade, so each viewing was a shadow of the last.

Just as she was watching a faint wisp of white evaporate to blue, her reverie was broken by a rousing fanfare from the top of the steps. She turned around to see Harold, cheeks puffed and face red, blowing into a bugle. Then he gestured to the French doors with both arms.

"And now… for the birthday cake!" he announced, like a ringmaster introducing his finest acrobat about to perform a breathtaking leap from a wire. A moderately flustered and pink-faced Hyacinth promptly tottered onto the patio presenting a cake smothered in pastel blooms on a shiny silver tray. Then she carefully tiptoed down the steps to the garden as everyone started singing "Happy Birthday", and continued to pad beneath the pompoms towards the table.

"Many happy returns my darling," she whispered, before placing the tray gently before Esme. The cake was tall and round and thickly iced in flowers of lilac, baby pink and cream. It was enough to make Esme's heart cry with joy. She closed her eyes, blew out a single candle and made a wish. It was the same wish she'd made on this day for the past ten years. Then she opened her eyes.

"I love it," she said, gazing up at Hyacinth who was beaming back down at her lovingly.

"It's the most beautiful cake I have ever seen. Thank you ever so much Mrs Hayes. I really am incredibly touched."

Hyacinth shook her head as if it was nothing and gave her shoulder a gentle squeeze.

"And thank you," Esme added, turning to her friends at the table.

"This afternoon has been completely magical. You've been so

kind to me. I really don't know what to say."

Daisy, who had managed to sleep right through the song, suddenly uttered the word "cake", which made everyone fall about laughing. Hyacinth started to cut the cake into fat slices, revealing a fluffy light sponge, with a thick layer of buttercream. Then Summer sprang up from her chair.

"Which brings us to stage two of the celebrations," she announced jubilantly.

"You mean there's more?" replied Esme, somewhat nervously. The Hayes family had been so wonderful to her over the years. She couldn't imagine why they offered such limitless generosity and often felt a little shy when they did.

"Well of course," replied Summer rolling her eyes, as if she ought to be used to her party planning with its layers of surprises by now.

"For we shall not be taking cake at Riverside Cottage, we shall be eating cake in Christ Church meadow where *you* will receive your presents!"

"My goodness. Now I really am speechless," laughed Esme, trying to take it all in but starting to feel dizzy. She put it down to eating too many sugary scones in the sun. Hyacinth, who sometimes struggled to keep up with her family's frenetic hospitality, was now hastily wrapping up slices of cake in tissue paper, then placing them into a Fortnum and Mason picnic hamper which had been hidden under the table cloth. Daisy, who had now been woken by all the activity, was scrutinising her mother's every move, poking the tip of her tongue out the side of her tiny mouth.

"Oh yes and remember to save a bit for Aristotle Mummy. You know how much he loves it," Summer insisted, referring to the family's white peacock, who had been casually wandering the patio throughout the day. Then Harold swiftly scooped up the picnic basket, and spun around with a belting:

"Get a wriggle on troops. Can't keep the other woman in my life waiting!"

Before marching up the garden in giant strides, then through the house and straight out the front door. Gathering up their skirts and chasing after him, laughing riotously, the girls eventually tumbled out onto the driveway. Harold was already sitting waiting in the front seat of his beloved 1930s MG motor car: 'Primrose'. He'd bought her from a dealer in Somerset as a retirement present to himself and spent as much time polishing her as he did listening to the shipping forecast on Radio 4. Hyacinth had welcomed the purchase, saying she'd have divorced him for being "humourless and predictable" if he'd taken up golf instead.

Since Harold had already checked the forecast three times today Primrose was proudly waiting with her roof down. She had cream leather seats inside pale yellow bodywork, which made Esme think of lemon meringue pie, and a silver grill with round headlamps popping up either side, which reminded her of Harold's moustache and glasses. He'd already strapped the picnic basket to the back and was wearing a jaunty straw fedora.

"Well climb in then," he bellowed, to which the girls clumsily clambered into the back seat, chattering and giggling all the way. Then he switched a key and fiddled a few knobs and levers until Primrose took off at such speed it made Summer's straw boater fly off into the driveway. Then they twisted and curled through the Oxfordshire countryside, laughing with their hair flowing, towards the towering turrets and spires of the city.

A little while later, Primrose pulled up in St Aldates by the entrance to Christ Church College, receiving numerous nods and smiles from passers by. Harold hopped out, opening the back door for the girls, before unhooking the picnic basket and handing it to Summer. She gave him a gentle kiss on the cheek and said:

"Thank you Dad, for everything, you're the best."

Harold adored each of his three daughters. But Summer's free spirit and boundless kindness had always been special to him. She'd arrived in the world shortly after his beloved mother Alice had left, and he found their natures refreshingly alike.

"All part of the service, me lady," he replied softly, docking his fedora and giving her a wink.

Then the girls wandered down the Broad Walk towards Christ Church Meadow, turning right onto its plush green expanse when they reached the walls of Merton College.

"Hmmm, right here ought to do it," said Summer, plonking the picnic basket in what she thought was the perfect place: just far enough from the colleges to feel "foresty", but close enough to have a "fabulous backdrop". She placed her hands on her hips to survey the location properly.

"Yes I think this will do just fine," she announced with great satisfaction. Then she opened up the basket and pulled out a lambswool blanket which she spread on top of the grasses and daisies below. The girls clambered on, kicking off their shoes and sitting with their legs tucked to one side, just as the bell of Christ Church's Tom Tower rang seven.

They heard the sound of a live jazz band strike up nearby. Then huddles of students, wearing white-tie and gowns, started drifting down the path towards Christ Church. Summer caught Esme watching them with a curious expression on her face.

"It's the May Ball ball tonight," she whispered to her friend, whose eyes were still fixed on the men and women in their finery.

"Christ Church's turn to host the commemoration ball."

Esme, lost in her own thoughts, smiled and nodded.

"I know," she murmured.

"How wonderful that must be."

Summer had known Esme since primary school, where they'd bonded over their starring roles in the Nativity play. Esme had played a modest Virgin Mary to Summer's effervescent Angel Gabriel, whose exuberant flying scene had led to an unfortunate incident involving a shepherd and a donkey. Summer had always been the more confident of the pair. But Esme, as is so often the case with only children, liked spending time with grown ups as much as people her own age. Summer knew how much she longed to be at university with her head in books and dressing up for parties, like she'd seen her Mum and Dad do in old photographs. Watching her oldest friend admire the students in their evening dress made Summer flash an involuntary grin.

"Right then missy. Without further ado, it's time to give you your presents..." she said, making Esme snap out of her day dream with a blush.

"But Summer you've already given me so much already," she insisted, gazing back with sincerity.

"The tea party and the cake were just so lovely. There really is no need to give me anything more."

"Oh codswallop!" Summer retorted, sounding a lot like her father.

"You know I love nothing more than to throw a tea party. The pleasure really was all mine. And I always like to keep the celebrations going for as long as possible, which means..."

She dug her arms into the picnic hamper and routed around for a moment or two. Then she pulled them out to reveal a bottle of Bollinger champagne in each hand.

"Summer!!!" exclaimed Esme, her eyes wide with shock.

"Where on earth did you get those?"

"My Dad's wine cellar," Summer said smugly, arching an eyebrow and sticking the tip of her tongue out.

"It's always stocked full ready for the next Hayes soirée. He'll never miss them. And even if he did, he'd happily turn a blind eye for your birthday bash."

"But we're only 16…," Esme said, biting her bottom lip.

"Oh who gives a stuff?" Summer went on rolling her eyes.

"It's not as if it'll be the first time. I was absolutely weaselled at my parents' 30th wedding anniversary and everyone, including Mum and Dad and the local vicar thought it was hilarious. Plus I know full well your Dad lets you have a nice glass of Merlot when you're having one of your cheese fondue nights on the rooftop."

Esme heard a cork pop and Summer was filling up cut glass champagne flutes, before she could further protest. She delicately handed them out, with an affected "For you, and for you". Then picked up her own, leaving her pinky finger out as if she were still drinking tea.

"And now for a toast," Summer proposed grandly, before clearing her throat.

"To our precious Esme on her sixteenth birthday. May she always be as sweet as she is wise. And to us, the glorious Goddesses of the Forest. Here's to a lifetime of adventures!"

The girls clinked their glasses with a joyous "A lifetime of adventures!" which reverberated across the meadow, followed by ripples of their laughter. Summer and Priya promptly knocked back their heads, taking a refreshing mouthful of cool champagne. But Esme tapped hers hesitantly against her lips, looking shyly from one to the other. Summer grinned back at her, her eyes sparkling with as much mischief as her champagne bubbles. Then she simply mouthed one word:

"Drink!"

By the time the bell of Tom Tower had struck eight they were onto the second bottle and things were starting to get a little noisy.

"Then Uncle Bob said it was the size of a cat, but I said I haven't even got a cat!" squealed Summer in hysterics. The others were creased over, crying with laughter, though neither of them really understood the punch line... which somehow made it even funnier. Three large slices of birthday cake had been devoured, with sticky crumbs and icing sugar spread across the blanket. Wiping away tears of euphoria with a greasy hand, Summer stretched her arms over her head like a ballerina.

"Right. Since Thomas has spoken, I believe it's time for the piece de resistance. Your third and final birthday present!"

"What?" mouthed Esme, shaking her head in disbelief.

"Oh yes, there's more...," said Summer, nodding happily, before handing Esme an envelope with a gold border and her name. It was damp, smelled of flat champagne and the writing was smudged.

"What's this?" she asked quietly.

"Well why don't you open it and then you'll find out?" Summer said, rolling her eyes again with a chortle.

"Oh come on Brains do keep up," she added impatiently, using the nickname she'd chosen for Esme on account of her sensible head and natural intelligence. Esme blinked at them both for a moment, then tentatively opened the envelope. She reached in and pulled out three small pieces of card. Slowly turning them over she let out an audible gasp.

"Who are these for?" she asked, turning the cards over and back as if looking for an answer, then looking from Summer to Priya in confusion.

"Well derrr," said Summer.

"They're for us three Brains. Who the hell else do you think they're for?"

Esme, with eyes agog, slowly read out the following words:

"This ticket admits one person to Christ Church's Commemoration Ball. Come join us for a night at the Circus you'll never forget."

Looking back at the girls, her head cocked to the side in confusion, she went on:

"But we're not…"

"Students?" butted in Summer.

"Well of course we're not silly. I got Honeysuckle to sort it out. She bought the tickets, then added us to the guest list under the names of three girls who she knows for a fact won't be going to the ball. So tonight, for one night only, we are Ruby Von Cuthbertson, Darcey Hornbuckle and Florence Rosenthall. See. It's genius. You're not the only one around here with brains you know, Brains."

Summer's older sister Honeysuckle was a third year law student at Christ Church and something of a cult icon to Esme.

"Kind of ironic that someone studying law should do something so gloriously illegal," said Priya with a mischievous grin, always the first to spot a moral quandary, but far too excited to care right now.

At the word "illegal" Esme felt her panic rising, while Summer calmly topped up their glasses with more champagne.

"I've got it all planned out," she carried on breezily.

"I thought it might be best to avoid the early rush. You know what I mean? Can't stand queues. So I made sure we'd have enough fizz to keep us going until Tom strikes nine. That's when we dust ourselves off and head for the main entrance on St Aldates. You let me do the talking. Then Fanny's your aunt, we'll be on our way to a night we shall never forget!"

Esme didn't doubt it would be memorable, though barely dared imagine how and why. She'd lost count of the times Summer had managed to get her into trouble at school with her incessant chatter and mischievous pranks. She'd once been threatened with detention after Summer put a kipper in her bag, which made her scream so loud it made their teacher Mr Finn scream even louder, slide straight off his chair and hide under his desk. But with a warm buzz beginning to spread through her body, and secretly longing to see what was behind Christ Church's towering walls, she crinkled up her freckles and said:

"Oh what the hell. Why not."

The other girls bounced up and down with excitement shouting "Yay!" clinking their glasses once again. Then they continued to drink freely and laugh wildly in the openness of the meadow, imagining what adventures might lie ahead on a night they would never forget.

## Chapter 4 - The May Ball

Five minutes after Tom had struck nine, three girls were waiting in a short queue beneath Christ Church's bell tower, trying not to fidget. They watched older men and women confidently hand over their tickets, before having their names scratched off a list. Then they vanished under Tom Tower and through an opulent pair of red velvet curtains draped from an arch on the other side. Esme's palms were clammy and her stomach was doing flips. She glanced at Priya, trying to read her face to see if she was having second thoughts too. But since Priya was the kind of person who could look composed in a sand storm it was impossible to tell either way.

"I don't know whether this is such a good idea after all," Esme whispered, glancing at the dour looking bowler hatted porter on the door. He had expressionless eyes and a mouth turned down like a trout. The sight of him made her tummy do another lurch.

"I'm sure it'll be fine," Priya cooed back, in a voice as smooth as a swan, giving her arm a gentle squeeze.

"This is the start of your lifetime of adventures, remember…"

Hearing the word "adventures" Summer, who was standing on her tiptoes trying to catch a glimpse of what lay beyond the velvet curtains, immediately spun around.

"What's all this? She's not thinking of bottling it is she?" she demanded, looking incredulously at Priya then suspiciously at Esme who was forcing an anxious grin.

"Look. Now come along Brains. When have I ever let you down?

It's going to be *fun!*" she went on, hoping her affected cheer would appease her.

"And you seriously need to get out more. Especially now you're sixteen. There's a whole wide world beyond the four walls of your Dad's barge you know."

Esme looked at Summer, who was nodding and grinning like a Cheshire Cat, and realised there was no point in arguing. Summer would never knowingly let her down, although most of her plans ended in hilarity, calamity, or both. The distant jazz music was now loud and clear, along with ripples of laughter and clinking of glasses from beyond the curtains. There was no turning back now.

"Fine," she said, rolling her eyes and shaking her head with a resigned smile. Although she looked about as "fine" as if she'd agreed to skydive.

In what felt like a matter of seconds the girls were standing in front of the porter's clipboard and pen which looked almost as boring as he did.

"Good evening Sir," said Summer politely to the sullen man, whose face remained impassive.

"We have three tickets to your fine ball."

Esme inwardly cringed. Summer's enthusiasm was enough to charm most. But the porter's bland face suggested she'd already over cooked it and blown their plan.

"Names," said the porter, in a voice as dull as his expression.

"Well I'm Ruby Von Cuthbertson," Summer lied, pronouncing the name extra carefully and clearly.

"And this right here is Darcey Hornbuckle and Florence Rosenthall."

The porter stared at each of them in turn, eyes dead, face

never flinching. Then he looked down, swiftly scratched three names off the list, before flicking the end of his pen and bleakly shouting:

"Next."

It was as simple as that. There were no trick questions, no formal identifications, and as Esme quickly realised, no escape! Summer grabbed the other girls' hands, squeezing them as tight as she could, as they tiptoed towards the velvet curtains. They were all holding their breath in case the porter should suddenly rumble their scheme and change his mind. As they drew closer, they spotted large white feathers fluttering in the gap.

"Here we go!" Summer chirruped gleefully, as if they were in a space rocket preparing for liftoff. The feathers were quickly whipped away, revealing two sequinned burlesque dancers, presenting a wonderland ahead.

The girls silently mouthed "Wow" as they entered a sparking scene of acrobats and circus entertainers within the castle-like walls of the quad. The jazz music they'd heard from afar was now all around as suited saxophonists, trumpeters and bass players wove around them. There were men in striped trousers juggling on stilts and giant illuminated animals from lions to elephants. They jumped as a bare chested fire eater blew a plume of flames in their path and marvelled at a woman in a leopard print bikini with an albino python.

"*Never* let it be said that I don't bring you to the best parties," said Summer, beaming at the fun and decadence, while plucking a glass flute from a passing tray.

Women in sequined leotards with feathers on their heads, were wandering between guests, with silver plates of champagne and canapés. And a dance floor around an extravagant central fountain had a burlesque dancer swinging above it from a giant helium balloon.

"Right follow me," Summer said, sounding like her military father again, before disappearing in the direction of fairground music. The other girls made their way after her, dodging through the crowds, until they found her in a carriage dangling from the bottom of an old ferris wheel.

"Well come along then. We haven't got all day," she insisted with an impish grin, shuffling over to make space. The others happily climbed in, gripping onto the safety bar as soon as they were locked in, before they began their ascent.

"This is literally the coolest place I've ever seen," said Priya, gazing at swirling performers and elegant guests getting smaller and smaller, as their carriage climbed its way up, gently rocking them back and forth. They could see the whole of Oxford lit up for the night, looking like a fairyland from above. Literally on top of the world, laughing every time her tummy went over, Esme wondered if life could possibly get any better than this. After going round and around for a few minutes, they finally heard the wheel's tinkling organ music drawing to a close, and their cradle steadily grinding to a halt.

"Right follow me," said Summer, the second they were back on solid ground, before vanishing back into the crowds. Esme and Priya wove their way through the vibrant quad: past a bejewelled acrobat blowing giant bubbles and a magician making a woman's glass of champagne vanish under his top hat.

"There she is," said Priya, spotting Summer just before she disappeared into the college's covered cloisters. They followed the tail of her long lemon dress, fluttering through long passageways lined with stone arches, until they found her at the bottom of a beautiful white staircase.

"Isn't it just the most exquisite thing you've ever seen?" she gushed with eyes glistening as she cast them up elegant stone stairs soaring beneath a dramatic ceiling fanning out into wheels. Huge gothic lamps stood like night watchmen at the bottom. While the refined sound of a string quartet at the top signified they were leaving the noise of the circus behind.

"Wow. It's absolutely gorgeous," exclaimed Priya, following Summer up the marble smooth steps, running her fingers lightly up the balustrade with her olive silk gown trailing behind like gloss.

"It's just like a palace," Esme sighed, floating through moonbeams piercing through tall leaded windows on her way up. Of all the things she'd expected from her sixteenth birthday, feeling like a goddess at a sumptuous, grown up party, certainly hadn't been one of them. She swung her dress lavishly as she twisted round a corner, feeling like the belle of the ball, as she made her way to the top. Approaching the string quartet she caught the pleasing hum of adult conversation and the tinkle of glass and silverware rippling through a huge wooden doorway. Summer was standing waiting, uncharacteristically patiently, like a footman at Buckingham Palace.

"Welcome... to The Grand Hall," she announced regally, with a solemn bow of her head, introducing them to the gentrified scene within.

A spectacular dining room with three sweeping tables of glamorous guests appeared beneath a vast hammer beam ceiling. Ancient scholars looked down from rich oil paintings casting their knowing eyes upon the youthful faces below. Stained glass windows with iridescent arches soared overhead.

"It's just how I imagined it," Esme whispered, in awe of the men and women clinking glasses and laughing at witty retorts in their elegant white tie and gowns.

"Oh look. There's Honeysuckle and Barney!" Summer squeaked, making a group of diners glare disapprovingly as she waved animatedly to her sister. Honeysuckle, a slightly older version of Summer with ice blonde hair swept back with pearl combs and a slinky silver gown, was sitting at the top table with her handsome boyfriend. They shone like the Snow Queen and King hosting a banquet. Summer quickly gave the pair a thumbs up to confirm their plan had worked and watched them radiantly raise their goblets back. Then she swept another champagne flute from a passing tray and tottered swiftly down the staircase back to the fun of the circus.

Esme and Priya soon found themselves back in the crowds, trying to keep up with Summer, who was heading towards the sound of a live band in another area. Eventually they found her hopping around at the back of a vast swathe of people cramped and swaying in front of a stage.

"It's the Blue Banshees!" Summer squealed above the noise, urgently beckoning them over.

"Come on, let's get to the front."

The girls shrugged at one another, then made their way after Summer, who was already squeezing her way through the crowd. After a little pushing and shoving and some disgruntled faces, they were at the front, gazing up at a four piece rock band. There was a beefy man with tattoos and a bandana sitting poker faced behind a drum kit; a waifish woman in a tie dye mini dress with a pixie haircut playing an electric guitar; and a man in a sleeveless t-shirt with hair gelled into spikes like a hedgehog, spreading spidery fingers across a keyboard. But Esme barely noticed any of them.

"Who's that?" she asked Priya, as casually as she could, with her eyes firmly fixed on the lead singer. He had a deep, soulful voice, with a slight crack in it, and was singing a moody rock ballad which she couldn't quite place. Moved by its slow, repetitive, haunting melody she softly started to sway.

"Ahhh the delectable and infamous Rafferty Montgomery," Priya purred, flicking her hair and moving gracefully to the music.

"The youngest son of Viscount James Montgomery the fourth.

They own a sprawling castle up in Scotland with tonnes of priceless artworks. The value is almost as eye watering as the stories about the family's debauched lifestyle. Seriously, their parties are the stuff of absolute legend."

Esme was only half listening. Rafferty had piercing blue eyes framed by thick black eyebrows and a stubbled chiselled jaw. He was cradling the mic stand in both his hands and singing down into it, his curls falling around his face. Esme thought she could sense melancholy in his eyes, and though she knew she must be imagining it, when he looked up from his mic, it felt like they were staring right at her.

"Oh my God, look at Summer!"

Esme's enchantment was brutally interrupted by Priya elbowing her in the rib.

"She's completely smashed. I think we need to get her out of here."

She spun around to see Summer hanging off the neck of a smug-faced man they didn't know. She was drunkenly wagging her finger at an angry woman in a silver tiara and a long crimson dress.

"Well heee never told me he was yoouuur boyfriend," she was slurring, prodding her finger towards the face of the woman which was rapidly turning as red as her dress.

"And anyways..."

Priya was now forcibly removing Summer's arm from the man, while the woman glared at them both with her hands on her hips.

"What's it to you anyway? It's not like you're married or anything."

"Come on now Summer. Let's leave these nice people alone," Priya was saying calmly but firmly, prising her away and rubbing her back.

"I think it might be time we got you a drink of water, don't you?"

Esme took one last look at the band before reluctantly following Priya and Summer out of the crush into an open space in the quad. Summer was standing with her back to her, wobbling unsteadily, wagging her finger at Priya who was trying her best to hold her up. She could still hear her slurring:

"I'm definitely not drunk Bambs. *Definitely* not drunk. It's just that my reality is a little different to yours right now..."

She saw Summer straighten up, shake her head a few times, before prodding her finger repetitively into Priya's shoulder:

"And with a little bit of luck that hopefully means that you're not seeing what I'm seeing right now..."

Priya spun around to see the trout-faced porter in the bowler hat, marching towards them, followed by two scowling women in peach and green taffeta ball gowns.

"Right then you lot," he said flatly, his tone still void of any personality.

"These ladies here reckon that they are Ruby Von Cuthbertson and Darcey Hornbuckle. So which of you is telling porkies?"

Summer, Priya and Esme glanced at one another nervously, before looking sheepishly back at the porter.

"Right, that's it. I'm going to have to ask you all for your college ID cards."

The two taffetered women instantly opened their clutch bags, dipped gloved fingers in and presented their cards, glaring triumphantly at the girls. Esme was chewing her bottom lip while Priya flicked her hair staring calmly at the porter with her hand on her hip. Summer, who was still wobbling, was urgently fishing around in her bag mumbling:

"Yes I know it's definitely in here somewhere. *Definitely. In. Here. Somewhere.*"

She was playing it so cool Esme half expected her to whip out three false IDs there on the spot. But instead, she simply clicked her bag shut, looked from one girl to the other, then shouted:

"*Run!!!*"

Summer turned on her heel and pelted off, leaving the others running as fast as they could to keep up. They kept losing her, as she dodged in and out of the crowds, until she ran back and grabbed their hands.

"Come on, I know a shortcut," she shouted breathlessly.

The girls scampered after her, through twisting hallways and secret gardens until they were finally back in Christchurch Meadow, hurling themselves onto their picnic blanket, screaming and howling with raucous laughter.

"Oh my goodness. That was absolutely *Brilliant!*" cried Priya, hugging her ribs which were aching from laughing so much, with tears streaming down her face.

"The look on those girls' faces. And that man. It was impossible to tell if he was happy or sad. I knew we wouldn't get away with it for long!"

"But it was all *so* worth it," gushed Summer, stretching her fingers and toes as she rolled across the blanket in delight, before pushing herself up on her elbow.

"I just loved it! What great fun. I'd do it again in a heartbeat. The circus, the dancing, the champagne… What about you Brains? Did you love it? Oh please tell me you loved it."

Esme was lying on the blanket gazing up at the stars, with her heart still pounding and her head in a spin. There was something about the night sky with its enduring jewels that gave her a sense of security when life was moving quickly. But the way that they were twinkling tonight made her feel something else entirely. They were like effervescent champagne bubbles, or sparkling trapeze artists, or perhaps even those eyes... Those eyes that felt like they were looking straight into her soul. Before she'd had a chance to answer, the sky erupted with streams of coloured rockets, spinning wheels and bright explosions, as dozens of fireworks shot beneath the stars. Slowly turning her head towards Summer, who was still looking at her intently illuminated by a shower of cascading lights, Esme smiled and said:

"It may well have been the best night of my life."

## Chapter 5 - A Missing Part

Esme wasn't sure if it was champagne or excitement that caused her to wake up with a sore head in her little room on the barge the next morning. But she rolled onto her back with her brow furrowed, wishing she hadn't drank so much. Hesitantly opening one eye she saw a deep blue sky scattered with silver stars and a moon, which she'd painted on her ceiling when she'd first moved to the barge. They'd helped keep her childhood memories alive of gazing at the night sky through her father's telescope in the garden of their beloved old house.

"Even though we have to move on, little one," her Dad had said, as she'd packed her favourite clothes and a couple of soft toys into a tiny suitcase.

"The moon and stars will still be up there waiting for us, exactly where we left them."

Gazing up at them this morning brought back new memories: of all that had sparkled from the night before. It made her smile and let out a contented yawn.

She'd lived on the barge with her Dad since she was ten years old. Her father, a lover of fixing things up, had bought the vessel from a boat yard near Binsey Village. Then he'd restored it, reconfiguring the layout to give both of them small bedroom spaces. Esme loved her little porthole by her bed which gave her a view of the ducks and riverboats passing by. She'd piled her mattress with a dusk pink eiderdown, covered in a patchwork quilt and a crochet blanket to keep her warm. Despite protesting that she was too old for toys, she still kept a teddy called Eddie and her old rag doll Violet at the end of the bed beneath a large watercolour she'd painted of Oxford's Bridge of Sighs. There was a long oval looking glass, mottled slightly around the edges, on her bedroom door. Glancing at the wooden boards below, she instantly spotted something new. It was a small cream envelope, with beautiful green writing spelling out her full name: *Esmeralda*. So few people ever called her that, it caught her by surprise.

She immediately swung her legs out of bed and padded over a shag pile rug, which tickled the soles of her feet. Then she picked up the envelope, perching on the edge of her bed to admire its swirling italics. Steadily turning it over she saw a red wax seal, and rubbed her thumb across its melted surface. Then she tore it open and pulled out a plain white card. Opening it she read the following words:

"I felt that I was leaving part of myself behind, and that wherever I went afterwards I should feel the lack of it, and search for it hopelessly, as ghosts are said to do, frequenting the spots where they buried their material treasures without which they cannot pay their way to the nether world."

How curious she thought. There was no "Dear Esme", nor a signature at the end. Yet something about the words resonated.

"The nether world…"

That phrase went round in her head. This idea of a hidden place of darkness underground. An afterlife, or perhaps even a former life now unreachable. She thought about the well at the heart of Teddy Hall and how she would gaze into it as a child, imagining a world below. How her father had told her bedtime stories to the same effect: Alice in Wonderland, Enid Blyton's Far Away Tree, and his own made up tales of magical worlds. She thought about buried treasure and the hunts her father had made in the garden of the large house in Oxford's Summertown where they'd lived. Before money had become tight and they'd been forced to downsize to the barge. And she thought about loss: something which sadly she and her father knew all too much about.

Rubbing her eyes and yawning again, she smelled coffee and eggs coming from the kitchen. As her tummy responded with a rumble she stood up and pushed her bedroom door open, plodding sleepily into the heart of the barge: a cosy wood lined space, painted soft cream, with three round portholes down each side. A soft glow radiated from a wood burner above a sheepskin rug, visibly worn where she perched for warmth, with a cashmere blanket strewn to one side. Her potted plants bookended well-worn paperbacks stuffed onto wooden shelves, with the family's old tabby cat Buttercup curled up in a wicker basket below. And her many watercolours patterned the walls below floral bunting, made from her old dresses, which snaked down the ceiling in a zig-zag. A violin concerto drifted from an old radio above the intermittent sizzle of a frying pan where Esme's Dad was preparing breakfast.

"Morning petal," he said, looking up from scrambled eggs he was stirring on an old cast iron stove. His glasses were lightly steamed and his apron was stained with coffee.

"And how is my grown up girl today? Are we officially a signed up member of the Goddesses of the Forest?"

Andrew Drake had chuckled when he'd seen Summer's invite propped against a jug of daffodils on the kitchen table. He'd watched the girls play dress up together since they were little and it tickled him that they were still as whimsical today as when they were small. He felt indebted to the Hayes family who had always treated Esme like a fourth daughter, knowing he couldn't offer her the conventional family set up they were fortunate enough to have.

"Oh I had the most wonderful day," she replied dreamily, kissing him on the cheek then leaning against the cupboard where they stored their pots and pans.

"Summer and Priya threw me an amazing tea party at Riverside Cottage. We sat under the big tree by the river, watching the world go by, with Daisy fast asleep at the table. Hyacinth had made sandwiches and macaroons and the most incredible birthday cake you've ever seen. The garden was dressed up with pompoms and I even spotted Aristotle wandering around. The whole thing felt like a dream. Then Mr Hayes drove us to Christ Church meadow in Primrose."

"Ah ha…" her father chuckled.

"So Harold's still knocking around with his other woman is he?"

"Oh yes. Still pootling around in Primrose like Mr Toad. Peeping his horn in his straw hat. Singing sea shanties as he goes in his big booming voice. He does make me laugh."

"Yes. He's a good egg that one," replied Andrew.

"And then what? After Harold dropped you off at the meadow?"

"And theeen."

Esme bit her lip, staring at the bunting overhead, choosing her words wisely.

"Then we just sat on a picnic blanket and ate birthday cake for a couple of hours, until it started to get a bit chilly."

"Ahh righty ho."

Andrew glanced over his spectacles looking a little underwhelmed.

"So it wasn't a late night then? I didn't hear you come in. I half imagined you lot might be partying the night away somewhere. I know things can get a bit lively when Summer Hayes is involved."

"Oh no Dad it was all pretty civilised."

Esme twirled her hair around her finger keeping her words to a minimum. Her father was relaxed in his parenting and she rarely lied to him. But she felt bad for breaking university rules and didn't want him to worry.

"But you saw the fireworks right?" Andrew continued, his eyes fixed on his scrambled eggs which were starting to congeal nicely.

"Christ Church always puts on quite the show," he added, just as the frying pan let out another loud hiss.

"Well of course," Esme replied, her face instantly brightening at the memory.

"They were fantastic. So kind of the university to organise them for my birthday!"

They chanted the last line in unison and laughed, repeating a joke the family had recited for years since, as a child, Esme thought the May Day balls and their fireworks were put on especially for her.

Andrew had brought Esme up alone ever since her mother Sienna had vanished when she was just six years old. He'd sometimes struggled with the responsibility of bringing up a girl, his own understanding of women being somewhat limited. However his adoration for her never wavered and he'd often marvelled at how this delightful young woman could have turned out so well, given the time he was also obliged to spend focusing on his students. Watching the freckles crinkling on her nose as she'd giggled at their joke, standing barefoot in her nightie, she'd looked just like the little girl who used to follow him around the garden, chasing dragonflies and making up fairy stories. But Andrew was well aware that his only daughter was growing up fast before his eyes and already held a wisdom well beyond her years.

"Right you are," he said smiling softly, his blue eyes twinkling behind his spectacles.

"Well as long as you had a good night petal. Now sit yourself down. Breakfast is served."

Behind them was a fold out table with wooden stools which he'd found at a thrift store and Esme had painted. She pulled out a duck egg blue stool, scuffed around the edges, and perched herself down. The tabletop was white with forget-me-nots around the edge and a jug of bluebells and lily of the valley sat in the middle. Yesterday's birthday cards arced like a smile from a string of red wool above. Esme was still clutching the card she'd found on her bedroom floor as she sat down. Andrew put two plates of scrambled eggs on toast, topped with freshly cut chives, on the table before her.

"I see you got your card then?" he said, sitting down and pushing his spectacles up his nose.

"Someone left it for you in my pigeon hole. I picked it up this morning after listening to the choir. Beautiful handwriting whoever sent it. Was it another birthday card?"

"It didn't say actually," Esme said drowsily, placing it open in front of her Dad. His eyes scanned the words as he poured coffee from a cafetière into mugs.

"Hmm," he said, trying to remember where he knew the phrase from before vigorously slicing into his breakfast.

"Ah yes," he said eventually.

"It's from Brideshead Revisited that. How original," he chuckled.

"Ahhh that's where it's from," said Esme, nodding as she made the Oxford connection. She knew the classic book was set in the city in the early twentieth century and made it sound particularly romantic.

"I've heard so much about it and how wonderful it makes life around here sound. But I've never actually read it, you know. I wonder why somebody would have sent it to me?"

"Hmmm I wonder...," her father replied.

"Well those were the words of Charles Ryder. After he'd spent a summer with the Flyte family, then life had dealt him a few ups and downs. It's what he said as he left Brideshead Castle, where they lived, for the last time. I suppose he was leaving his memories of his younger days behind. So perhaps that's why. Quite apt for your coming of age really. Strange that no one thought to sign it though," said Andrew.

Esme nodded in agreement as she chewed on her breakfast.

"It was probably just some amorous student," Andrew went on, giving her a roguish grin.

"It's actually still quite popular with my second years studying twentieth century literature. Or it might just be a promotion you know. New editions pop up in Blackwells from time to time."

Esme took the card, glancing briefly at it again, while sipping her coffee.

"So what's on the agenda for today?" Andrew added, in a mock official tone.

"Are we planning to steal a Renoir from the Ashmolean Museum? Or break into the Bodleian Library? Or just be boring and head to the gardens as usual?"

When Esme wasn't painting or reading she loved spending time at Oxford's Botanic Gardens. Her mother was passionate about botany and her father had proposed to her there when they were just twenty one years old. As a working class boy from the north he knew the beautiful and aristocratic Sienna Blythe was completely out of his league. But nevertheless she'd eventually fallen for his warmth and good humour; as well as his sharp intellect and their shared love of Victorian to mid century literature. He'd saved up for six months to buy a first edition of her favourite book which he'd had delivered to her on their wedding morning at her parents' lavish Berkshire home, Avaley Hall.

"Boring I'm afraid," Esme replied over her coffee cup.

"It's back to the gardens for me today. I've promised I'll help Dougal in The Conservatory. Then I'm meeting Freddy for coffee."

"An afternoon with Freddy eh? You'd probably be safer stealing the painting!" Andrew teased. Esme rolled her eyes, nodding back in agreement.

"But it looks like a lovely day for the gardens… Say hello to Dougal from me."

Andrew took a mouthful of coffee then stifled a loud yawn with his fist.

"Oh excuse me," he apologised groggily, shaking his head to wake himself up.

"My long night's catching up with me a bit. I should probably have a quick nap. I'm off to watch the Maypole Dancing in Radcliffe Square later."

Esme almost spat out her coffee.

"Maypole Dancing!" she exclaimed, with eyes almost as wide as her coffee cup.

"Now that's a first. You're not thinking of taking it up as a hobby are you Dad? I can't really see you skipping around the street swishing your handkerchiefs. Although I do think you'd look rather lovely in a floral hat…,"

"Hey now pack it in you," he laughed, playfully poking her arm for taking the Mickey out of him.

"There's about as much chance of me Morris Dancing as there is of Dougal taking up break dancing. So don't you worry. There'll be no fear of that. I just promised a friend that I'd go there to watch them, that's all. Then I'm popping down to London for a book signing. I probably won't be back until late. Will you be alright fixing yourself up some grub later?"

"A friend…" Esme thought. Apart from Dougal she wasn't aware that her father had too many other friends. It made her sad to think that he spent so much time devoting himself to his students and she couldn't bear to think of him being lonely. For a moment she wondered if this dancer might actually be a female "friend". Her father was still a nice looking man and she knew of at least two students who had a crush on him, with his scholarly mind and laid back charm. Although it secretly broke her heart to think of him with anyone other than her Mum, she knew he'd eventually meet somebody and would benefit from the company. She smiled lovingly back at him.

"Yeah sure Dad. I can sort out dinner. We've got plenty in. I was actually thinking of making one of my spaghetti bologneses. I'll leave some in the fridge for you to heat up when you get back."

Andrew looked up from his breakfast with eyebrows raised in approval.

"One of your legendary spag bols eh? Mmm, I can taste it already. Thank you, my love. You certainly know how to look after your poor old Dad."

Andrew felt blessed that his daughter had turned out so nurturing and thoughtful. But it still made him feel guilty that she'd had to grow up so quickly, making up for his mediocre domestic skills in the absence of a mother.

"You're an absolute angel. Or should I say goddess?" he added with a grin, unable to resist one more joke about Summer's fanciful entertainment.

Despite Andrew's best efforts Esme was generally the cook and cleaner on the barge, looking after her father as much as he did her. Ten years since her mother had disappeared she knew her father still ached with the loss. Rumours had circulated for years over her whereabouts. Some claimed she'd returned to her blue blooded roots and ran away with a viscount, while others believed she'd drowned herself in the Cherwell River after becoming depressed as a struggling author. Despite the fact that police divers had searched it several times. Some students even claimed to have seen her ghost floating through the cloisters of Magdalen College late at night. Though such suggestions were generally put down to too many hours spent with their heads in books or in the college bar.

Sienna's parents Lord and Lady Blythe, or Michael and Priscilla to their friends, had initially blamed Andrew for her disappearance. They said it was his late nights spent reading or marking essays that had driven her away. However they'd continued to worship Esme, who bore a striking resemblance to her mother, and eagerly looked forward to her visits. Until they suddenly passed away within six months of each other just a few years after their daughter vanished.

Andrew worshipped Esme and had tried his best to shield her from the whispers, reassuring her that her Mum had loved them both deeply. Spending time at the Botanic Gardens made her feel closer to her. Plus she loved learning about the flowers and their properties from Dougal, an old friend of her parents who still worked there. As a little girl she would bring armfuls of cornflowers and marigolds home from the meadows and pretend to cast spells with them. She'd even dress as a miniature witch with Buttercup, who was just a kitten, as her magical sidekick. Her mother's copy of The Language of Flowers was still in the barge and Esme liked to imagine her reading it when she took it from the shelves. But for now it was just herself and Andrew and the little life they had made for themselves on the river.

She stood up and ruffled his hair as he drank his coffee and started leafing through a newspaper.

"Right, I'd better be getting off. Have fun in London. And be good. Love you," she said, lightly kissing the top of his head.

"You too Petal. You too…" he replied, quietly marvelling at how much it was possible to love another human being. Esme wandered back to her bedroom with a full stomach and an even fuller heart, thinking how lucky they were to have one another.

## Chapter 6 - A Small Box

The sun was blazing down on the Thames by the time Esme left the barge. Dressed in dungarees, with a ponytail tied up high with a red polka dot scarf, she stepped onto the front deck before her boots jumped onto the mossy towpath. She heard a familiar cry of "pull" as eight men whizzed by in a rowing boat, droplets dripping from their oars like pearls as they sliced through the water. Then she paused to admire the barge's glossy bodywork as it glistened in the sunlight. Her father had painted it a golden mustard to which she'd added poppies, marigolds and lilies down either side. A row of red hearts ran just below the roof, while the barge's name, Perditus Amor, swirled in blue inside a garland of forget-me-nots at the front. Esme spotted Buttercup sunbathing on the roof and shouted:

"See you later puss!" to which she received a nonchalant twitch of an ear, before swinging her satchel over her shoulder and heading off.

Walking past university boathouses, taking care not to collide with a line of students marching with their rowing boat held aloft, she turned onto a tree lined footpath. She smiled and said Good Morning to tourists balanced precariously on punts on the Cherwell River threading alongside. After following its twists and turns for some time, the broad expanse of Christ Church Meadow rolled out to her left. Docile cows were munching grass while willows and wildflowers swayed in the breeze. How soothing it seemed without the champagne laughter and crackling fireworks of the night before. It wasn't long before the turrets and spires of colleges began to rise like castles in the clouds on the skyline. Esme imagined all the secrets from centuries of balls hidden in their walls. Then taking a left onto the busy High Street she was finally at her destination.

She loved striding through the solid stone archway to The Botanic Gardens to be greeted by the delicate tranquillity within. A fountain poured softly into a pond surrounded by pristine lawns and nurtured borders. There were meandering paths lined with mossy urns, and a walled garden with ancient trees and medicinal plants. Esme walked a short path, alongside a pair of eager ducks waddling towards the river, to the grand glass Conservatory.

There were a number of Victorian glass houses at The Botanic Gardens. But Esme particularly loved The Conservatory with its exotic fruits and fragrant flowers. Quietly opening the door, humidity hit her face and earthy, citrusy scents filled her nostrils. Creeping towards a familiar mop of silver hair, bent over a hydrangea bursting with lilac pom poms, she whispered "Morning" as softly as she could.

"Great sparks!" said the mop, spinning around to reveal a narrow face with ruddy cheeks and tiny startled eyes, magnified by oversized glasses. It was attached to a small man in a brown apron, worn over a green woolly jumper with patches on the elbows. One hand was spread across his chest while the other brandished a pair of secateurs.

"Oh thank goodness," he gasped, audibly exhaling as he gradually lowered his weapon.

"It's only you. Must you always scare the living daylights out of me Esmeralda?"

Dougal Flint was one of only a handful of people, including her head teacher when she was in trouble, to use Esme's full name. He was a restless man in his sixties, who had always suffered with his nerves, which is one of the main reasons he'd taken up gardening. He said that he found the orderliness of maintaining the shrubbery "meditative" and the aromas a "tonic to his senses". Esme had known Dougal since she was a little girl and loved him like a family member. His detailed knowledge of botany was exemplary and she enjoyed listening to him reciting the plants and their Latin names. And she always tried her best not to scare him. But since he'd been known to jump at the sight of a ladybird this had proven an arduous task.

"I'm so sorry Dougal," she said kindly, with eyes full of concern.

"How are we doing today?"

"Well apart from people sneaking up behind me to scare me out of my wits," he replied with a disgruntled nod in her direction.

"I can't complain, can't complain. Although…"

Here we go thought Esme.

"This warm weather does bring out my allergies, something terrible and my back's playing up. But you know me," he said, his speech gathering speed as it usually did.

"I have to keep soldiering on or else no one else around here will. And then that would be that. Five hundred years of botanical history up the spout."

He broke off abruptly, pulled an inhaler from his apron pocket and drew on it with a loud wheeze.

"Oh we know, we know," Esme replied, forcing her face into the most serious expression she could muster.

"This place would fall apart without you and we are all *so* lucky to have you," she added, squeezing his arm affectionately.

"Ah get away with you," he said, brushing her off with a shy grin and reddening cheeks.

"Now come and give me a hand getting those dahlias planted, while I try not to have a coronary. You can tell me what you and that know-it-all father have been getting up to."

Esme obediently followed Dougal past pygmy pineapple trees and potted chilli peppers towards an empty flower bed on the other side. She knelt beside him as he started digging holes with a trowel, passing him bulbs from a bucket to plant one by one.

"Dad's been really busy with his students lately Dougal," she said, once they'd gotten into a flow.

"I've barely seen him actually. But he's off to London today. Apparently there's a book signing he's interested in."

"Is there now?" he replied, looking up and blinking rapidly behind his thick glasses.

"So I suppose that's why he cancelled our Friday wine night last night is it? I had a feeling he was up to something sneaky. As well as getting up at some God awful hour for that choir I suppose."

Esme said nothing, just smiled and nodded. She felt relieved she hadn't mentioned the Maypole Dancing to Dougal. Not to mention her father's mystery friend. His requisite for order meant he wasn't fond of change and his nervous disposition made him highly suspicious of new people. But Esme was still extremely touched that his Friday nights with her Father still meant so much to him after all these years.

Dougal had known Andrew Drake since he'd helped him organise his proposal to Sienna at The Botanic Gardens twenty years ago. The men discovered they shared a love of fine wines, as well as a lack of close friends, so their bond had become extremely important to them both. Dougal loved nothing more than to discover a new vintage to share with Andrew at the barge. He'd arrive promptly at 6pm, smartly dressed, sporting a brightly coloured cravat and a bottle wrapped in brown paper tied up with gardening string. Andrew would bring out the crystal wine glasses he kept wrapped up in a box under his bed for special occasions. Then the pair would head to the roof where deckchairs would await, and quaff and converse until the stars came out. At which point it was customary for Andrew to bring out blankets, followed by a tray containing cigars and cut glass tumblers of whiskey, with which to round off the night.

Conversations during these evenings would generally start with their verdict on the wine, which they usually agreed on. Then switch to literature, horse racing or politics which they rarely ever did. But there was a singular topic which was strictly out of bounds: a woman who they had both loved and still missed everyday. Watching Esme in The Conservatory, her fine bone structure looking more elegant by the day and her steady gaze revealing a maturity beyond her years, Dougal thought he could have been looking at his old friend Sienna.

"Oooh that reminds me," said Dougal snapping out of his thoughts.

"Now it's not much, but I have a little something for you. Now don't get too excited, you know my nerves can't take it. It's just something and nothing that's been lying around for some time. So I thought I might as well give it to you as anybody."

He reached into his apron and fished around for a while. Then he pulled out a small square box, wrapped in brown paper tied up with gardening string. He blushed before handing it to Esme. She paused hesitantly, a little taken aback.

"Lovely Dougal, you shouldn't have," she said, gazing down at the carefully wrapped cube in her palm. Then she started to unwrap it.

"No, no, no, stop!" he blurted.

"Save it for later dear. I told you not to get excited. You'll have me coming out in hives at this rate."

"Ahhh right you are Dougal," said Esme softly. She slipped the box into her satchel and said no more about it.

The pair worked quietly for the next hour, gently tending a

bounty of flora and foliage, spilling from pots and creeping up glass in the elegant Conservatory. Esme often wondered what Dougal got up to when he wasn't at The Gardens or sitting on the roof of her barge drinking wine with her father. She remembered visiting his little thatched cottage in Witney as a child, where he'd treated her to banana sandwiches and lemonade in the garden. She'd been captivated by his dusky walls covered in old botanical drawings and his ordered vegetable patch, with a tame robin hopping around his wellies waiting for him to upturn a juicy earthworm or two. He'd never been married. And despite his tireless attempts to keep the inside of his home under control it was always a little chaotic. Just like Dougal himself. As far as Esme knew he didn't invite her dad there anymore. He preferred to focus on the important task of sourcing a new Chablis or an old Malbec and taking it to Perditus Amor. She smiled as she thought what an unlikely pair they were with their weekly ritual, yet what a genuine bond they'd developed over the years.

By the time Esme had begun carefully pruning the citrus trees, Dougal had gotten into his stride, offering some of his finest botanical facts.

"Ahhh yes the Tree of Life," he said sagely, gazing up into the branches of a mandarin tree.

"So much more than just a spiritual concept. You know, that force that connects us all. With its infinite cycle of life and death and so on and so forth. Because the Tree of Life is actually a map which scientists have been working on for decades. To show how everything on earth is connected. It's like a diagram, if you will. With branches showing the evolutionary relationships between plants and animals. And every other form of life."

Esme was busy plucking dead leaves from a tree but nodded to show she was listening.

"Of course Latin has been the primary language of botany for

2,000 years," Dougal went on, as he began snipping away at a rose bush.

"And each plant is given two names you see. First is the genus, and second is the species. It's fairly simple once you get the hang of it. You know like *Rosa rubiginosa* he said," holding one of the flowers aloft.

"Red rose," said Esme, instantly recognising the name. She broke into a smile seeing Dougal with the same flower.

"Yes very good, very good," he said, bobbing his grey bob in approval.

"And not only do these names help us place them within the Tree of Life. By letting us compare their similarities and differences. They also help us understand the fundamental characteristics of the plant. You know, like *Digitalis purpurea*. Which translates as purple digits for foxgloves."

Esme smiled imagining long purple fingers bursting with bell-like flowers. The Latin names really did help you picture them, she agreed.

"And then that's where things start to get really interesting," Dougal went on knowingly.

"Because botany, where a name expresses the very nature of something, now starts to reveal a very close relationship to…"

He looked furtively from left to right.

"Magic…" he said, in a manner which was both mysterious and grandiose.

Esme stared at Dougal with her eyes wide with wonder. He blushed and quickly shifted his focus back to his roses. Esme's mind drifted back to her childhood. She thought of casting her spells with Buttercup using flowers from the meadows. *Maybe it wasn't just a game,* she thought, feeling somewhat spellbound herself. *Perhaps magic really was… real.*

A little while later, having carefully potted pink hyacinths and finely sprayed the palms, Esme tiptoed up to Dougal. He was sitting on a bench beneath a bay tree, making a list of plants in need of replacements.

"Dougal," she whispered, perching beside him, folding her hands in her lap.

"Do you mind if I ask you a question?"

Having watched Esme hang on every word during his short botany lesson, Dougal looked up from his notebook, his spectacled eyes wide with anticipation.

"Why of course dear," he replied, his voice uncharacteristically calm.

"You can ask me whatever you like."

"Well," she went on cautiously.

"I hope you don't mind me asking. It's just a silly thing really. But you know. My Dad hardly ever talks about her, and my grandparents are no longer here. Plus I know that the two of you were friends and she used to come here and help you. So I was just wondering. Can you tell me what you remember about my Mum please?"

Esme fell silent, looking at Dougal longingly as she waited for an answer. The air in The Conservatory was balmy, yet Esme suddenly felt goosebumps on her arms. Dougal's flush had gone from his cheeks and his eyes had lost their expectancy. His glasses looked like goldfish bowls, as his eyes started swimming, searching for an answer. But they didn't look at Esme. They finally rested on his fountain pen, placed in the spine of his notebook, still open in his lap. Then Dougal drew a breath and solemnly said:

"A finer rose these gardens never did see."

And that was it. The Conservatory fell silent again, bar the silvery notes of a robin, perched outside in a magnolia tree. Without looking up Dougal picked up his pen and continued writing his list.

# Chapter 7 - Freddy

Esme was still worrying that she'd upset Dougal when she left the gardens later that day. He'd looked so sad when she asked him about her Mum and remained pale and withdrawn ever since. She knew that, apart from her father, Dougal had few friends and that Sienna had once been very dear to him. She wondered if perhaps she shouldn't have brought her up. Still worrying, she turned onto the High Street and made her way the short distance towards Queen's Lane. She stopped short of heading up to her Dad's college, calling at the quaint coffee house on its corner instead. Despite being hundreds of years old, it was now a laid back cafe, with sumptuous cakes and pastries in glass display cases, and wall to wall windows under chocolate coloured awnings. She ordered a pot of tea and a raspberry tart to cheer herself up and took them to her favourite spot: on a little table by a bow window overlooking the High Street. She normally came here at least once a week, sometimes to meet friends, but more often than not just to people watch.

She saw off-track tourists pausing outside the elegant Grand Cafe opposite to study maps, and students artfully dodging around them, trying not to spill arms full of books. Many wore caps, gowns and stoic expressions as they turned down the road towards the grand Examination Schools. She imagined how they might be feeling as they climbed its marble staircases then poured out years of study beneath ornate ceilings. How she longed for the day she might be just like them. Although the pressure to follow in her parents' footsteps and gain a place at the university sometimes weighed heavily on her.

She knew a lot of her Dad's college's students by name and liked to live vicariously through them. She spotted Rosaline Carmichael, a twenty year old from the Home Counties with the looks of a country lady crossed with a model. Her slim frame sashayed past the window, with poker straight blonde hair flowing down her back. She was wearing a black cashmere polo neck tucked into skinny jeans with black ballet flats. A miniature handbag stretched across her body on a long strap, which Esme assumed was probably designer. While two interlaced Cs were attached to her ears, which even Esme recognised as Chanel, despite her limited knowledge of expensive brands.

As she turned the corner onto Queen's Lane, Esme heard a shriek and spun around to see Rosaline through another window being swooped up and swung around by a well built gent. By contrast to her understated elegance, he was wearing scruffy jeans, tucked into calf high army boots and a knitted jumper full of holes which hung off one shoulder. He flicked his dark curls away from his face to reveal piercing blue eyes which Esme recognized straight away. Then she watched the man she had found so captivating on stage at the ball, place Rosaline safely back down before she punched him playfully in the shoulder. He ruffled up her perfect hair, threw an arm around her neck and then the pair staggered off like drunk teenagers towards college.

Suddenly the cafe door sprung open and Esme nearly fell off her chair as a voice shouted:

"Caught you. Stalker!"

Before she knew it she was being poked and tickled around her middle and a splendid head of Afro hair was burrowing into her neck.

"Gerroff me Fred," she squealed, wriggling and pushing her best friend, Freddy de Villiers, away.

"You love it," he said, grinning back roguishly.

"Lucky it was me who caught you staring and not Lord Lustalot."

"Freeed!!" she shrieked, trying not to laugh.

"You're completely bonkers."

"Well that's because all the best people are babe. Isn't that what you always say?"

"Yes I do, Freddy. That *is* what I always say," replied Esme, laughing since it was indeed one of her favourite retorts.

Esme had known Freddy ever since he'd turned up in short trousers with a pinstripe blazer and a tiny briefcase at her infant school at seven years old. Priya was the first to spot that this beautiful young boy, with a halo of black hair, wasn't included in the other boys' games, and was being cruelly taunted for his South African accent. Pained by his big sad eyes, and remembering how difficult it was to fit in as the new girl, she immediately asked him to join their gang in the playground. At first this had led to even more teasing for being "a girl", until Summer stamped it out by putting glitter glue on the bullies' chairs. Esme could still remember the look on Wilburt Shufflebotham's face, as he tried to explain to their teacher why his own bottom had turned purple and sparkly. Finding Esme crying over her missing Mum in the cloakroom shortly afterwards, Freddy had comforted her, and the pair had bonded after he shared how he'd come to England a few weeks before with just his Mum. With the help of his new friends, Freddy gradually grew into the popular and flamboyant young man sitting before her, with a love of fashion as relentless as his endless hunt for fun and salacious gossip.

Esme took a long sip of her tea, as she wondered whether Freddy might be able to provide her with a little bit of tantalising information of her own. Sensing him twitching with expectancy as he tried to read her thoughts, and knowing he was like a walking Who's Who of members of the aristocracy, she decided to bite the bullet.

"So you know him do you?" she asked nonchalantly, casually flicking her eyes in the direction of the window.

"Who? Lord Lustalot? Rafferty doo dah? Who doesn't!' Freddy exclaimed emphatically.

"His family are completely loaded and utterly mad by all accounts. And him and that Rosaline whatserface are basically the college soap opera. Supposedly crazy in love but off more than they're on, thanks to Rafferty's many distractions. You know rugby, rugby drinks, that grungey band of his and all the pretty groupies that go with it."

"Riiight," said Esme, feeling slightly crestfallen but grateful to Freddy for keeping her in the picture. Blissfully unaware of his friend's disappointment, Freddy pushed his chair back, leapt up and did a theatrical twirl, swinging his arm above his head like he was wielding a sword.

"Anyways… what do you reckon?" he went on, gesturing up and down his body which was clothed in a tight cream t-shirt, navy chinos and a burgundy Liberty scarf tied in a sophisticated knot around his neck. Freddy had got into brands and style long before he started doing a spot of teen modelling and was always impeccably turned out.

"Don't tell me," replied Esme, screwing her eyes up as if she didn't already know the answer to this recurrent game.

"You've been working out and are almost at your ideal holiday weight?"

"Bingo!" he said joyously, clicking and pointing both fingers in her direction.

"Now that right there is why *you* are my very best friend and why I shall buy us both a peppermint tea by way of my never ending gratitude. We simply must have tea."

Esme knew that was the right answer to almost any question Freddy asked her. She watched as he fluffed his hair and flirted with staff behind the counter before strutting back, hips swinging, holding a tray aloft on one hand. He placed it on the table in front of her saying "Pour Vous", in an exaggerated French accent. On it were two steaming tea cups, along with a long flat parcel wrapped in white tissue paper tied with a gold ribbon with a small white envelope tucked inside.

"Happy Birthday darling," he said warmly, leaning down and planting a kiss on the top of her head.

"Oh Fredster," she said, wrapping her arms around his neck, so grateful he was here to cheer her up.

"Well hurry up and open it then!" he said, unwrapping her arms and flapping his hands impatiently towards the gift, as he took the seat opposite. She picked it up, opened up one end and pointed it towards her other hand. A cerise pink scarf slid cooly into her palm with a satisfying swish. She took two corners between her fingers and thumbs and carefully opened it out to reveal a square of pure silk. A mystical Indian scene unfolded before her eyes of an exotic tree with a delicate twisting trunk and fine branches smothered in red-white blossoms and blue-green leaves. Enigmatic peacocks stood at its base and then fanned their tail feathers overhead.

"It's like a work of art," Esme gasped, taking in the intricate design, with its border of fruit and flowers resembling an ornate picture frame.

"Well of course it is. It's Liberty daaarling," Fred said airily, sitting back and crossing his legs as casually as a fashion editor.

"Thought it was about time we spruced you up a bit. And I know you're always banging on about flowers and such and such. Plus that thing in the middle is the 'Tree of Life'. It's the name of the scarf. Since you are now officially ancient I thought that seemed appropriate too."

"The Tree of Life. How curious," mumbled Esme thinking how strange it was that Dougal had also mentioned it earlier.

"Oh Fred I absolutely love it," she went on happily, pulling the polka dot scarf from her hair and swiftly replacing it with the Liberty one.

"Ta dahhh," she said, folding her hands under her chin and pouting expressively towards Fred.

"Simply gorgeous," he said approvingly, clapping his hands delicately like he was in the Royal box at the ballet.

"Now we just have to get you out of those scruffy dungarees and old boots and Lord Lustalot will be yours for the taking."

"Freddy Stop!" she scolded, through a fit of giggles.

"Oh you love it!" he said, winking then licking his tongue out as she covered her face and tried to conceal a fit of giggles.

Once Freddy had filled Esme in on the hottest school scandals, including which friend had had a nose job and who was secretly dating a lecturer, he air kissed both her cheeks, said "Ciaow" and left the cafe with his customary panache. After staying out late, plus a generous helping of unfiltered Freddy, Esme's head felt fuzzy and her limbs were heavy. But since her Dad was out of town she decided to swing by the college and check his post.

It was almost dusk, but this was always Esme's favourite time to visit Teddy Hall. Walking up Queen's Lane, then turning right into its front quad, she gazed up at its rectangle of old buildings. She loved watching the tiny leaded windows, peeping out of the wisteria, light up one by one and imagining what might be going on inside. Academic geniuses who would be awake until the early hours poring over classic books, or free spirited students playing music and drinking wine before heading out. She wandered past the old dining room and saw long tables laid with fine silverware and candle sticks awaiting guests. She imagined waiters opening silver domes to reveal sumptuous food, and glamorous men and women making one another laugh with witty remarks and clever anecdotes. Then she glanced into the low beamed bar, and saw its fire roaring with students huddled over pints of beer and cider. She wondered what they might be talking about: philosophical musings on the meaning of life perhaps, or how old one should be before tackling James Joyce's Ulysses. Or did these students just discuss things like who the best looking rugby player or the prettiest fresher is? Her thoughts were broken by the sound of high pitched laughter and a clatter of heels as three girls with long hair and short dresses tumbled out of a stone staircase. The scent of their perfume hung in the air as they swept past Esme and off out into the night.

Yawning, she remembered why she had come to the college in the first place, and wandered back to the porter's lodge.

"Evening Mr Frogmore. How are you today?" she said brightly, as she hopped up the steps towards the pigeon holes.

"Oooh you nearly caught me nodding off there," said Mr Frogmore sleepily.

"It's been a long day, and my chilblains are playing up, and now I'm back here again for the night shift. Wish me luck. Happen you're here to pick up your Dad's post are you? Haven't seen him around since this morning."

"Yes please Mr Frogmore, that would be great, he's gone to London today."

"Right you are love, you know where his pidge is," he said dozily, putting his open newspaper across his face and leaning back for a snooze.

Walking up to her Dad's pigeon hole, she saw a pile of letters poking out. She quickly grabbed them and was about to put them in her satchel when she suddenly felt the air cool and her scalp bristle. Out of nowhere she got the sensation that she was being watched. She quickly spun around and caught the tip of a black cape sweeping past the entrance to the lodge. It made her freeze to the spot with an uneasy sensation. Then remembering that being tired always made her paranoid, she rubbed her eyes and wrinkled her nose. It would just be another professor turning up for the formal meal she thought. Taking a deep breath to calm herself she glanced down at the post she was holding. And that's when she saw it: a small cream envelope with her full name written in distinctive green writing: *Esmeralda*.

## Chapter 8 Protection

Esme woke up early the next day. After feeding herself and Buttercup the night before the pair had quickly dozed off together in front of the fire. She was woken just after midnight by a gentle shake of her shoulder from her father who had crept into the barge on his return from London. Then she'd snuggled beneath the eiderdown on her bed and fallen into a heavy slumber until the first light of morning started peeping through her porthole.

It was 6am, and her Dad was still fast asleep, when she crept into the barge's living space. She put the kettle on the stove and made herself a cup of tea along with two slices of toast smeared with thick layers of marmalade. Then she wrapped a blanket around her shoulders, grabbed her breakfast and satchel and made her way onto the roof.

There was nothing Esme enjoyed more than the peace and tranquillity of the river at this time of the day. Settling herself into a deckchair she wrapped her long fingers around her steaming teacup and silently soaked in the scene. A pair of swans swam serenely alongside a duck, drake and five tiny ducklings lined up in a row. She watched a moorhen, beak full of branches, busily tending its nest and a bright blue kingfisher streak by to pluck a fish right out of the water. The sun was starting to peak above the treetops, and a light mist above the water was slowly rising.

With her head calm she reached her hand inside her satchel, and felt around for a moment until the rough string of the box brushed against her fingers. Then she pulled it out and placed it on her lap. It was the first time that she, or anyone else she knew, had received a gift from Dougal and she wasn't sure what to expect. It took a while to loosen the string which, ever cautious, he'd secured in an especially tight knot. But once she'd finally released it, the paper fell away to reveal a black leather box with a small metal clasp. She used her thumb nail to carefully prize it open and pulled back the lid.

Gazing up at her from a grey velvet cushion was a pendant. It had a delicate purple flower, with just two petals, pressed onto cream parchment paper in a gold oval frame.

She looped a finger under the chain and carefully lifted it up, watching the morning sun flicker across its surface like liquid gold as it twisted and turned.

"Wow. It's gorgeous," she whispered with genuine awe, marvelling that Dougal could have picked out something so exquisite. Then, spotting a piece of parchment paper neatly folded inside the lid, she pulled it out and read its short message:

"Baptisia for Protection"

D

It was written in erratic scribble which she was more used to seeing Latin plant names scrawled in on wooden markers. Yet the gift and the words disarmed her. Dougal rarely showed his softer side, so the fact that something so thoughtful had come from him touched her deeply. She fastened it around her neck, placed one hand over it, and felt a warm balm of relaxation flow through chest.

With her eyes closed she stretched a hand towards nearby herbs she'd rescued from offshoots from the gardens and planted in a cut down beer barrel. She rubbed lemon balm and mint between her fingers and felt their aromas sharpening her morning senses.

Then, she heard a creak of the barge followed by a deep northern voice saying "Come on then Buttercup,". She opened her eyes to see her cat followed by her Dad jumping onto the roof.

"Morning Petal," he said, padding towards her in pyjamas and a tartan dressing gown, pulled in around the waist with a college tie. His mousy hair was sticking up to one side as it always did when he'd enjoyed a deep sleep. He was clutching a newspaper and smelt of coffee and cigars when he bent down to kiss her, his morning stubble scratching her cheek.

He scooped up Buttercup, who had beaten him to his deckchair, before sinking down and placing the disgruntled cat back in his lap.

"Morning you. Good day in London?" she asked, smiling over at him.

"As London goes, not bad at all actually," he replied heartily, looking well rested and younger than his years this morning. He flicked his paper open and gave it a shake, before quickly scanning the headlines.

"Kept seeing an old student of mine, Charlie Tobin, popping up on the Sunday Times bestseller list. So I went to Piccadilly for one of his book signings to see what all the fuss was about. It's one of those gruesome murder mysteries set in far fetched extravagant locations with a million twists and turns. Not really my thing, but they're flying off the shelves, and it was splendid to see the old boy. Then I popped over to the Royal Academy to check out their latest Impressionists exhibition. There were some fascinating early sketches by Cezanne and Degas, it's well worth a look. Then I grabbed a quick bite on St James and made it to Victoria just in time to hop on the last train home."

Watching him chat away, leafing through the Sunday paper, Esme thought how rare it was to hear him talking about doing something nice for himself for once. He sounded chirpier than she'd heard him in a long time. She wondered for a second about his new "friend" and whether that might be the source of his new vigour.

"Oh did you get your post Dad? I left it on the table for you," she said, watching as his bespectacled eyes darted about the latest news events.

"I certainly did. Mostly bills, a few press releases and more bills. Oh and a not so subtle reminder from Mr Bartholomew that he 'very much looks forward' to seeing me at formal hall tonight. As if I'd dare to forget! But thank you all the same," he said breezily, the bulk of his attention now taken up by a story about a political scandal at Westminster.

The pair sat in silence, bar the rumble of Buttercup's purring, for a minute or two. 'Formal Hall', thought Esme. That was unusual for her father too. She knew how much he disliked stuffy events, particular sit down dinners where there was little room to escape. And the pressure to bring along a guest always threw him. Perhaps he really had met somebody she thought. The idea filled her with a strange sensation, somewhere between sadness and relief.

"And how was your day?" he continued, changing the subject with a rustle and a turn of a page.

"Did you catch up with Monsieur Fred? Manage to get a word in edgeways?"

"Have you and Fred actually met?" she joked, rolling her eyes, pleased to be back on common ground.

"I can categorically say I did not. But I could probably now write a dissertation on who's been selling knock off designer bags. So that's a win. Oh yes and I saw Dougal," she continued.

"You'll never believe what…"

She broke off abruptly. Her father had put down his paper, and was sitting upright in his chair. His eyes were fixed on her chest, with a mixture of pain and confusion.

"Daddy?" she said, using a name she rarely called him these days.

"Is everything ok?"

He reached forward and carefully lifted up the pendant, turning it slowly, a look of total bewilderment on his face.

"Where did you get this?" he asked quietly, his tone so vulnerable it made her chest ache.

"It was a birthday gift from Dougal. He gave it to me for…"

"Protection," he said flatly, finishing her sentence but never taking his eyes from the necklace.

"How did you…?" she continued.

Then realising that there was only one topic which could elicit such a bleak response she softly asked:

"Was it…?"

"Hers," he broke in stiffly, closing his eyes and taking a slow, deep breath. Then, without warning, the corners of his mouth turned up and an unexpected sound came from the pit of his stomach: laughter.

"Dougal, Dougal, Dougal," he chuckled to himself heartily.

"I can't believe the old boy kept it. Haven't seen that thing in years. Well I'll be blown. That certainly takes me back a bit."

Esme stared at her father, unnerved by his sudden gear change, with an urge to laugh too. But a feeling of emptiness took her over instead. Then a twinge of petulance. Anger almost. She felt like her Dad was keeping a secret from her, and treating her like a child.

"We never talk about her Dad," she said curtly, with her face serious and her tone direct.

"I would really appreciate it if you'd tell me more about her.

Andrew became sedate once again, with his face placid and his eyes soft. He placed his hand on Esme's, looked into her eyes and said;

"She would have been so, so proud of you."

Then he leaned back in his chair and closed his eyes with a faint smile, his eyelids flickering slightly like he were replaying a happy memory.

Then to Esme's complete amazement he continued on:

"It was Trinity term 1993, and I was studying for my Mods. I'd won a scholarship to Magdalen as you know, but I was still just a shy lad from Yorkshire who just so happened to love books. I spent most of my time at the Bodleian or at my desk in my room overlooking the deer park. I still had to pinch myself that I got to read the world's greatest literature with a view of something that looked like a scene from the Countess of Pembroke's Arcadia. If I threw open my windows I could often hear the college choir practising in the chapel. The way the sound echoed up from the cloisters was enchanting and made me feel like I was in heaven.

But I struggled when I had to sit down and mix with the other students at formal dinners. I was never comfortable wearing a gown and felt like an outsider next to these privately educated sorts who seemed to go way back and speak a totally different language to me. I didn't understand the rules of rugby or recognise the names of the schools they talked about. It was both one of the happiest but also loneliest times of my life.

Until the night of the May Ball. All of the popular students had bought tickets but, with little money and even less desire to make awkward small talk, I'd planned to just stay in my room and study. But, sitting in my window with a glass of brandy and a cigar, I heard the sound of the choir practising the Hymnus Eucharisticus they'd be singing from the top of Magdalen tower the following morning. It was the first time I'd heard it and I was completely and utterly mesmerised. To this day I'm not sure what made me follow the sound of the voices. But before I knew it I was standing in the doorway to the chapel. Then the music stopped and the choir picked up their belongings and left. All apart from…"

"Mum?" said Esme.

It was a word Andrew wasn't used to hearing from his daughter and it momentarily took him aback.

"Yes, the beautiful Sienna Blythe," he sighed.

"I crept into a pew and sat and listened as she continued to practise the hymn alone with a voice as pure as an Angel. With her gown hanging from her shoulders and her auburn hair framing her face she looked like a bird of paradise.

We locked eyes for a brief moment as she finished, before she swept out of the chapel and was gone. I barely slept that night. I couldn't wait for dawn and the opportunity to hopefully see her again, singing from the top of the tower."

"But hang on," said Esme. "I thought only boys sang in the choir on May Day back then?"

"Yes, but you know your mother," Andrew continued with a knowing smile.

"She thought that was all terribly outdated and unfair. So she struck a deal with a tutor that if she could top his paper on feminist literature, you know Simone de Beauvoir, Silvia Plath and the like, he would organise for her to secretly sing alongside them. She studied from dawn till dusk to make sure she achieved good marks. Then she pinned her hair under so it wasn't too obvious and that was that."

Esme's eyes grew misty with pride at hearing this. Of the many wonderful things she had learned about her mother, her fight for female equality was the thing that pleased her the most.

"It wasn't until a month later that I actually got the opportunity to speak to her though. I'd been invited to a scholar's dinner. I knew your mother had won a choral scholarship and would likely be there. So I slipped into the dining room early and swapped the place names. At first I was completely and utterly tongue tied and regretted my decision. But once she asked me what I was studying and we got onto the topic of Victorian literature that was that. She was the first person at the college I felt truly at ease talking to.

We were friends for a while first. She'd come to my room to hear my thoughts on poems she'd written and we'd wander around the deer park reciting Shakespeare sonnets. She even talked me into joining the drama society. We stayed in college the following summer after the other students had gone home, to perform in a production of A Midsummer Night's Dream. And that's when we grew closer. We'd take wine to the river after rehearsals and regularly still be up talking when the sun came up. And it was on the final night, while celebrating the production with the rest of the cast, that we shared our first kiss. We were interrupted when a cheer went up around us. It seemed just about everyone else had worked out we were in love.

Then as you know, less than a year after that, I popped the question. I told her that I'd bumped into Dougal who'd asked if she wouldn't mind popping into The BotanicGardens and helping him for an hour before I took her for a birthday lunch. Of course, being Sienna, she said she'd be delighted. But thanks to Dougal's help, I was already waiting under her favourite tree with a champagne picnic, at the end of which I got down on one knee.

A few days later he found the Baptisa pendant, which she never took off, under the same tree. But she handed it back to him, insisting he keep it by way of thanks for his help with the engagement surprise. In truth she had hoped its healing powers might help ease his ragged nerves. And today was the first time I have seen it again since the day I proposed to her twenty two years ago."

Then Andrew closed his eyes once more, with one hand resting on Buttercup's gently heaving belly, and leaned back into his chair. Esme's head was swimming with a million questions, but she knew now was not the time to push her father further. With her mind full of fresh images of her Mum, she wrapped her hand around the pendant and vowed that, just like her, she would never take it off.

# Chapter 9 - Hetty

It wasn't long until Esme heard a sound she was familiar with hearing on a Sunday after her father had read the paper: snoring. Then she crept discreetly along the barge's roof and slipped inside to get ready for the day. She pulled on a pair of jeans with a thin, grey sweater, smoothing her loose hair away from her face with Freddy's scarf. Perched on the edge of her bed by her looking glass she was pleasantly surprised by how it brought out her eyes. She curled a wand of mascara through her lashes and smoothed gloss across her lips which made her features glisten. Then she pulled the flower pendant out of her sweater so it lay prettily on her chest for all to see.

Grabbing her satchel she made her way down the river, breathing the morning air, thinking what a glorious blessing it was to be alive. She swung her arms to ease her body, which had remained still as a statue while her father was telling her stories about her mother. How Esme had longed for him to share more and wished that she could remember her a little better. Raising her eyes to the sky she prayed, as she did everyday, that one day she would come home.

It wasn't long before she spotted a snake of dense black smoke curling out of the chimney of a rundown barge. Paint which had once gleamed in black gloss had faded to ghostly grey, while flowers that had garlanded the sides were now worn down to morbid wreaths. A jumble of broken pots and iron kettles smothered the roof, bulging with more weeds than plants. While the mysterious name *Asphodel* hovered like a spirit in faint script towards the bow.

Esme instantly recognised this sinister vessel and always hurried her pace when she spotted it moored on the river. She had just reached the 'A' of Asphodel when a small figure dressed in a tatty grey sack leapt into her path.

"What's the big rush?" barked a low woman's voice, which cracked and wheezed as it spoke. It came from a face largely concealed by long black hair which was threaded with silver and as coarse as the mane of a horse.

"And on God's day too, I didn't have you down for a heathen," she continued to goad. Then she gratified herself with a rattling cackle.

"Now come here and let me take a proper look at you."

A skeletal arm reached out from the sack, wrapping gnarled fingers around Esme's wrist, while the other hand swept the curtain of hair from her face. It revealed woeful eyes set in a surprisingly delicate face with high cheekbones and a pointed chin. Her skin was so pale as to almost be translucent with lips that almost vanished into the flesh. And though her eyes were grey as the morning mist, they would occasionally flicker with iridescent violet. But right now they were bloodshot and watery as they scanned Esme's face with a vehement hunger.

"My, my, my, aren't we becoming quite the beauty?" the woman taunted, as her hand left her own tangled tresses to snatch at one of Esme's locks. Her fingers slid down it as if it were a ribbon of silk, with eyes following like it were gold.

"And just look at your crown of glory. Glowing like a burning halo. Just like Aphrodite's and Mary Magdalene's did before you. Those shameless sorceresses, carnal sinners, deceiving men through the lasciviousness of the flesh."

She was slowly pacing around Esme now, scrutinising her from all angles like a magpie eyeing up a string of diamonds from a tree. This mysterious woman's life story had become the stuff of local legend. According to folklore she'd once toured the world as a dazzling acrobat with her father's circus the Enchanted Big Top, before settling in Paris and becoming a can-can dancer with the Moulin Rouge. An accomplished ballerina, with the face of Audrey Hepburn, she was as renowned for her grace as her beauty, her beguiling violet eyes frequently compared to Elizabeth Taylor's. Watching her pace around the riverbank, with her knotted hair and ragged clothes, Esme found it almost impossible to picture her in her heyday.

"Let not the eye of a red haired woman rest upon you they say," the woman jeered, grabbing Esme's jaw and locking eyes with her.

"Those eyes. Those emerald jewels, more befitting of a rampant wood nymph. Shining from the Leviathan sea serpent like the glimmerings of dawn. Like Cupid's envy of Hercules, stealing Psyche and flying her away for his own wanton pleasure."

Esme's heart was pounding as she stood frozen to the spot, daring not to move. She'd caught glimpses of this woman over the years and had occasionally passed the time of day. But she'd never been this close or heard her speak in this manner. Her behaviour was erratic and unpredictable and Esme felt trapped and panicked. The woman's voice was getting louder and it was clear she was enjoying herself. Her eyes were burning with intensity and her lips were moist, revealing yellow teeth when they parted. Esme could feel warm breath against her skin and it smelled of boiled cabbage.

As quick as lightning, the woman let go of Esme's jaw, and leaned in close to her chest.

"And what's this I see?" she said with a gasp, grabbing the pendant and pulling it close to her eyes. She turned it over and back before nodding with recognition, speaking wistfully like a sage:

"Ahh the blue iris. The mystic baptisia. It would appear that you are smarter than you look my dear. Choosing an amulet for protection with a face as beguiling as yours."

Feeling the chain snatch around her neck, Esme's instincts fired up with primal protectiveness. After her father's recent revelations she felt more close to her mother than ever. She prized the woman's fingers off her pendant, shoving her away with both her hands.

"Get away from me Hetty," she cried out, using the only name she or anyone else she knew, had for this woman. She'd been appearing on the riverbank sporadically since they'd moved to the barge, and she felt as terrified of her now as she was as a little girl. Hetty cowered melodramatically for a moment before attempting to assuage Esme:

"Now, now. There's no need to be afraid of me, my dear. Hetty's only trying to protect you. Goddesses should join hands and form circles. To keep one another safe."

Then she closed her eyes and began to sway, gracefully sweeping her arms from side to side while quietly humming. Esme just about made out a discordant "ring a ring a roses". It made her feel sickly with its eeriness. She was about to make a run for it, when Hetty's eyes snapped open, blocking her path again in one giant leap.

"Now then," she continued, her tone more matter of fact now.

"I've got a pot of Wood Betony on the stove. Why don't you come in for a nice cup of tea? It could be just what you need to protect you from unwanted attention. To fight off any love spells some amorous fool may have cast on you."

Trying to make the offer sound more appealing, she went on:

"Now come along. It will just be the two of us. I could read your cards for you if you liked?"

It was only then that Esme sensed something in the woman's

tone she hadn't noticed before: Loneliness. Her fear and anger started to subside a little.

"I'm so sorry Hetty. I'm running a little bit late for my errands. Another time perhaps?" she said, as politely as she could.

Shaking her head furiously like a child, and refusing to take no for an answer, Hetty grabbed Esme by the elbow. She felt her heart start to race again, feeling foolish for trusting such a capricious character. Hetty started forcefully manoeuvring her towards her barge, scolding her like a school maam:

"Punctuality is the virtue of the bored my dear. Now come along. I've got a lovely Black Tourmaline I can spare you. Ought to be just the job to get rid of all this negativity you are carrying around with you. It's dreadfully ageing you know."

Esme was carrying a lot of tension, she must confess. But the last thing she needed was to be ensnared any longer by this crazed banshee. She used all her strength to prise Hetty away, stating loudly and firmly:

"I'm sorry I really must go. Bye Hetty," before taking off at pace down the river, leaving the other woman silently mouthing after her. Her once ravishing eyes were like sorrowful pools, swirling with fury and dismay.

According to the stories it was those eyes that captured the attention of a Hollywood film director in the clandestine cocktail bar of Paris' Maison Souquet: a lavish boutique hotel famous for its former life as a pleasure house. They fell passionately in love, and when he promised to cast her in his next movie, she followed him back to his Beverly Hills mansion, where she spent a blissful six months basking in his adoration. Until she fell pregnant. It was only then that the rumours of a secret wife who'd been studying in Italy started to emerge and the director eventually sent her back to Paris with a one way ticket. Little is known of what happened to the child, who is believed to have been a boy. But it's said that once he was born

Hetty vowed never to trust another man and to make it her mission to protect other women from their villainy.

As Esme continued to speed down the riverbank she heard Hetty's rasping voice screeching after her:

"Well have it your own way, you skittish little minx. You'll just have to learn the hard way!"

Esme kept running as fast as she could. But the image of those desperate eyes was impossible to outrun, following her far away into the distance.

## Chapter 10 - Rupert

Esme continued to run as she made her way alongside the Cherwell to the High Street. It was only once she reached this broad thoroughfare, with its soaring colleges, that she dared slow down amongst the tourists and Sunday shoppers. Flanked by palatial buildings, like Queens College with its rooftop cupola, and University College with its turreted gate tower, she felt protected by its stature.

Pausing briefly outside Oriel College, Esme caught the hallowed sound of Sunday hymns, drifting across the quad. Then after crossing the street she made her way to the historic covered market and its myriad of coloured shop fronts. Wandering beneath glowing lanterns and twinkling fairy lights, she breathed in musky aromas of lavender and rose from a nearby soap shop. She strolled towards a bright red post box, then through a doorway surrounded by spring blooms, into a store packed with freshly cut English flowers. She watched the wizardry of the florist's fingers weaving together soft peach roses, yellow poppies and sweet peas, before wrapping them in brown paper and placing them in a customer's arms like a sleeping baby. Then she picked up a thick wedge of Camembert for her father to enjoy with his port, and gingerbread tea for them to sip by the fire.

Once her shopping was done Esme ordered a colourful salad, topped with sunflower seeds, which she ate on a small table with a Mediterranean mosaic top. Then after ordering a cup of English breakfast tea, she reached into her satchel, and drew out the latest mystery envelope which she'd found in her father's pigeon hole. She placed it on the table and paused for a moment, running her hand across the perfect green letters spelling out her name. She simply couldn't place the writing at all, and had no idea why it had been sent to her. But she opened up the card inside and silently read its words:

"Sometimes, I feel the past and the future pressing so hard on either side that there's no room for the present at all."

"No room for the present…"

Could this be another reference to her birthday she wondered? She'd received lots of lovely gifts, but why on earth would there be no room for them? After all, the barge wasn't that small!

And how come the past and the future were pressing on either side? She imagined it must be a warning not to dwell on the past, nor to fear what might be ahead. She closed her eyes, took a deep breath in and out, and tried to focus on being in the moment. But just as she was starting to drift towards serenity, a loud clunk followed by the screech of a chair dragged her out of her meditation with a start. With her eyes still lowered, she saw a heart shaped tart plonked haphazardly on top of the card. A distinctively nasal and pompous voice followed:

"No need to panic, this isn't some sentimental declaration of love!"

It sounded like a train driver announcing an emergency detour through a loudspeaker. Then it followed its hurried statement with a nervous chuckle.

Knowing exactly who this voice belonged to, Esme begrudgingly raised her head. Sat before her was Rupert Delaware: a second year student who she had it on good authority from her Dad had developed a humongous crush on her, after she'd interrupted his tutorial to ask whether he'd prefer toad in the hole or shepherds pie for dinner. Known unimaginatively by his fellow students as "Rupert Bear", thanks to his penchant for a chequered trouser, he'd deposited his red and yellow slacks on the chair opposite her without waiting for an invite. His patterned bottom half was paired with a crisp white shirt, a tweed waistcoat and a purple dickie bow. He had limp brown hair to his ears, which parted down the middle and clung to his head like wet string. And his pointy nose, which he was never reluctant to poke into other people's business, was visibly twitching with excitement.

"Only me," he continued, like a whiny bus conductor attempting to sound easy breezy.

"A little bird told me that last Thursday was an important date."

Esme silently cursed her father who was undoubtedly said bird for inciting any more of Rupert's unwanted attention.

"So I bought you a delectable treat," he went on, nudging the tart closer, as if to elucidate.

"By way of saying Bravo, you know!" he declared with a triumphant grin and a flare of his nostrils. His prying eyes spotted Esme's card. He snatched it rudely from under her tart with another tetchy laugh. Hastily pulling on his spectacles, which were hanging from a chain around his neck, he silently read out the contents.

"Oh right, you are, I see," he said, leaning back in his chair and stretching his long legs, invading Esme's private space even further.

"A bit of Brideshead. Splendid stuff, splendid."

Then, with his nose actively twitching again, he spun it over and slowly read out two lines, which Esme hadn't spotted:

"To find out what it is you lack.

Go to where the books are black."

"Oh marvellous, I see," he said, putting his hands behind his head, squinting at Esme like he didn't really see at all.

"Somebody's sent you a riddle, what fun!"

Esme could hear the words her father had said on seeing the first card echoing back to her as Rupert struck his reclined pose, looking worryingly as if he was trying to wink at her:

"Probably just some amorous student. It's still quite popular with second years studying twentieth century literature," he'd said.

Could it possibly be Rupert who was sending her the cards she wondered with alarm? With her suspicions heightened she decided to cut to the chase and put him on the spot:

"So what do you think that means then Rupert?" she asked bluntly, studying his reactions like a hawk following a rabbit. He let out another awkward laugh:

"Well that would depend on what it is you lack now wouldn't it?" he chortled, as if he were pointing out the blindingly obvious.

"Anything you need my dear? An extra sausage for your toad in the hole perhaps?"

He looked enraptured by what he thought was their in joke before realising his double entendre and almost choking on his tea.

"Hmmm what am I lacking? What. am. I. lacking?" she mumbled, drumming her fingertips on her chin and sticking her bottom lip out.

"Well some new side fenders for the barge would come in handy," she added matter of factly, cocking her head and watching Rupert visibly recoil at her lack of refinery.

"Oh, and a clue as to what these cards are all about would be nice," she added, folding her arms and slumping back as if bored of the game.

"There's been more than one?" he enquired, flickering his

nostrils with genuine interest.

"Oh yes. There was another one. It was left for me on my birthday. That one had a quote from Brideshead Revisited in it too."

"Well there you have it then don't you," he declared, letting out an involuntary snort at his apparent genius.

"It sounds like someone's asking you to find the rest of the book. The bits you don't have are clearly 'what it is you lack'. You see!"

"Someone is seriously asking me to track down one specific book... *in Oxford*?" she groaned as if they were asking her to find a single grain of rice in the market.

"Well not every riddle has an answer," Rupert added mysteriously, which Esme thought was actually rather unhelpful.

"But buck up," he went on, like an enthusiastic boy scout.

"Because this is precisely where yours truly may be of service."

The next thing Esme knew Rupert had taken her fork from her hand, mid bite of her tart, and had wrapped her satchel across his chest. Then his long chequered legs took off down the market, while Esme zigzagged around shoppers trying to keep up.

"About turn," he hollered, with a flamboyant flick of his hand, spinning right at the exit onto Market Street, almost overturning a fruit and veg barrow.

He was leaping towards Radcliffe Square, with strides so long Esme half expected him to take off. She slowed down briefly to wave to a friend but Rupert immediately sprang back and grabbed her by the hand.

"No time for that!" he bellowed.

He was pulling her towards the most central square of the

city, finally slowing down and stopping once they were within spitting distance of its famous round library.

"The Rad Cam?" she asked perplexed, while trying to catch her breath with her hands on her knees. She slowly drew herself up, and looked up at its magnificent dome, soaring above elegant stone pillars set around a perfectly circular building.

"Well I think it might be pertinent to start at the beginning, don't you?" Rupert said smugly, before dragging her up a stone staircase to the entrance without waiting for an answer.

Reserved strictly for university students, it was the first time Esme had ever been inside the Radcliffe Camera. She meekly tiptoed into the centre and tilted her head towards its layers of arches and galleries, fearing that any moment she would be thrown out. But once Rupert had given a surprisingly smooth wink to a librarian, who nodded reassuringly at a security guard, the building was all theirs. Enthralled by this magical space, Esme stretched her arms out, turning her face blissfully towards bright rays of sun pouring beneath its ornate domed ceiling. Spellbound by all the bookcases circling her she started to turn contentedly around on the spot. Rupert quickly tapped her on the shoulder, and whispered loudly in her ear:

"Now there's no time for that!" pointing towards a large round clock whose hands were already at 4.30pm.

"Right you take the middle floor, and I'll take the ground. Think of it as bunking up," he said, like an excitable boarding school prefect.

"Only a bit of history on the top so nothing to see there."

"And exactly what are we looking for again?" she asked bemusedly.

"First we go to the sections where there are blocks of hardback books that are all black. And if they happen to be twentieth century literature then Bob's your uncle. Bit of luck, that's where we'll find the Brideshead," he instructed, thoroughly into Head Boy mode.

"Got it!" she said, with enough enthusiasm to cause a nearby student to loudly shush her. Then she quietly crept up a spiral staircase to the middle floor, and started the circular route within its bookshelves.

There were glass cases stuffed full of everything from Beowulf to Bronte, in every colour imaginable. She peered through each of them, twisting her hair and biting her bottom lip like she always did when concentrating particularly hard. But aside from the perfect symmetry of the architecture, little else appeared uniform. She spotted a block of the complete works of Chaucer bound in leather, but they were all in red. There wasn't anywhere immediately obvious where all the books were black.

Nearing the end of her circuit Esme started to feel disoriented, unsure whether she was back at the start or not. But spotting the top of the spiral staircase, she tiptoed back down, shaking her head at Rupert, who was already tapping his foot at the bottom.

"Zippo my end too," he said almost as vigorously as he was grabbing her hand.

"But don't despair. There's plenty more where that came from."

With that he whisked her through a door and down another winding staircase, until Esme mysteriously found herself standing in a bright white tunnel. It was lit up as luminous as a futuristic spaceship, with slick black stripes down either side. There was a door at the end which looked so far away it appeared that only elves would fit through it.

"Where are...?"

"The Glink!" Rupert interrupted, declaring the tunnel's name majestically while taking an uncharacteristic pause to admire its clinical and direct route.

Esme stared blankly at Rupert, baffled and none the wiser. Although the name had made her picture goblins underground in Harry Potter's wizarding bank: "Gringotts". She shook her head, releasing this wasn't at all helpful. Then she tried asking again.

"The what now?"

"The Gladstone Link," Rupert replied impertinently and impatiently, as if it ought to be perfectly obvious by now.

"Whizzes us right underground, and straight into the Bodleian Old Library. You know how I love a shortcut," he added with glee. Then his long chequered legs were off again, leaving Esme taking twice as many shorter steps as she tried to keep up.

After what felt like running a marathon through a rabbit warren, Esme finally found herself above ground in the oldest part of the university's library. She felt so tiny below the towering book cases made of ancient gnarled oak, she wondered if she had actually arrived in a wizard's study and been shrunk into a pixie. A stained glass window at the end of the cases appeared minuscule. Though she imagined it would probably soar above her head if she moved close to it. She was starting to feel quite overwhelmed, and imagined the leather bound manuscripts flying off the shelves, spinning around her like a whirlpool. Until Rupert, who had already started scanning the shelves, suddenly popped his head out, instantly jolting her back to earth:

"You do know that 'the Bod' contains every single book and publication printed in the country. That's around thirteen million for us to go at in here," he announced, as if that were a good thing.

"There's even a book made out of cheese!" he added ecstatically, twitching his nose at the thrill, until the look on Esme's face made him realise he'd finally gone too far.

"But where will we even start Rupert?" She moaned wearily.

"This is beginning to feel impossible!"

She didn't wish to sound ungrateful. But it would take about a hundred years to get through this colossal library and its miles of hidden tunnels, with old mechanics and long conveyor belts, operating like an underground book mine.

"Well we'll just start at the beginning again and then...."

Rupert's voice tailed off as he saw Esme's eyes drift towards the library's refined reading area where identical twin sisters had just arrived. They had shiny black bobs and matching clothes and were settling down at a polished table beneath identical table lamps.

"Ah yes," said Rupert, following Esme's gaze.

"Tamsin and Tamara Mountford from Brasenose. As identical a pair of twins as you'll ever see."

"No but wait, look," whispered Esme, pointing and gesturing for Rupert to watch more closely. Tamsin and Tamara were now sitting shoulder to shoulder taking brand new books out of matching bags. The shop's name, which was clearly in view, provided Rupert and Esme with the answer to their puzzle.

"Blackwells!" they mouthed to one another, while fighting the urge to jump up and down and scream. Rupert quickly looked down at his watch, mumbling:

"Drat! We're too late. It's almost six o'clock. But we might just make it if we hurry."

Esme, somewhat relieved by this get out, smiled and kissed him lightly on the cheek. It was a gesture which made him blush right up to his ears:

"Lovely Rupert," she whispered.

"You're the absolute best and I simply couldn't have done it without you. But I think we've both had quite enough riddle solving for one day. Don't you?" she added, patting his arm reassuringly.

"Plus there's no school tomorrow. Which means I can just pop to Blackwell's bookshop in the morning. Find out what's what then."

Rupert was trying hard to hide his disappointment at their vigorous bounty hunt being over. But he nodded back as graciously as he could, replying stiffly:

"It was my absolute pleasure and honour."

They turned and silently left the library, through a beautiful white hallway flooded with sunlight. It had a gothic stone ceiling which made Esme think of spider webs. Then they walked towards the Bridge of Sighs, and didn't speak until saying goodbye outside Teddy Hall.

By the time Esme made it back to the river the evening was crisp and she was looking forward to the warmth of Perditus Amor. Hetty's barge was no longer moored up and a beautiful sunset had turned the sky crimson and gold. Her legs were weary but her mind was calm and it seemed everything was back to the way it should be. She couldn't wait to wrap up in a blanket with Buttercup on her lap and drink gingerbread tea in front of the fire. Then she'd get an early night, so that she could arrive at Blackwells early and spend the rest of the day reading the book. Drifting past the occasional rower, lost in her thoughts, she didn't even notice her barge until she was almost at the entrance. But as she raised her eyes dreamily from the towpath a chill immediately shot down her spine. There was something attached to the vessel which wasn't there this morning. Her scalp started to prickle, just like it had when she thought she was being watched in the college lodge. And then the rising panic.

A bunch of dead roses was hanging from the bow with a Tarot card fixed on top with an opal hat pin. It had a ghoulish drawing of the Grim Reaper wearing a suit of armour, riding a white horse. Below it, in Olde English text, was the word: DEATH.

Esme snatched it up and turned it over to see if it came with a message. It did. There in front of her, scribbled in red ink, was a stark and sinister warning:

"Beware the Dark Stranger."

# Chapter 11 - Brideshead Revealed

Esme's body was burned out and her mind overburdened by the time she made it to Broad Street to visit Blackwell's bookshop. She'd tossed and turned until the early hours, her mind fuelled with fear and fury over Hetty's ominous threat. How dare she come to the barge when Esme had made it clear that she didn't want her cards read. Perditus Amour was *her* sanctuary, a private enclave, set apart from the world and its threats. Yet the comforting womb of her tiny bedroom had been ruptured by four chilling words: "Beware the Dark Stranger". She'd even sat up in bed, convinced she could hear Hetty's menacing cackle, before realising it was just the sound of a distant moorhen. And once her body gave in to exhaustion and fell into a deep slumber, haunting images of the Grim Reaper and the word DEATH still flooded her dreams.

But despite her sore eyes, the sight of the blue shop front, with its windows stacked with books below gold letters spelling out Blackwell, still managed to lift her spirits. Walking into its cavernous interior, with its layered floors and miles of bookshelves, took her back to her childhood. She would come here regularly, getting lost in the smell of new books and the endless adventures hidden within their covers. But today wasn't a day for arbitrary browsing, today she knew exactly what she was looking for.

The shop was quiet and Esme made her way straight to the Classic Fiction section, her eyes as focussed as an archer's, until they landed on B. Then she dragged her finger across the ridges of the hardbacks until it met its target. She paused and ran it up and down the spine, feeling the texture against her skin, before gently sliding it off the shelf. After instinctively riffling its pages beneath her nose, she held the book out in front of her. It was a beautiful, clothbound edition of Brideshead Revisited, covered in pale blue pools of ever decreasing circles. The sight of it made her chest flutter, just like standing behind the velvet curtains at the May Ball, waiting to discover a hidden world beyond.

She'd spent hours lost in fairy tales and romances in Blackwell's reading room over the years. But knowing exactly where she would take this particular book, today she went straight to the counter. As she drew close, a loud clatter followed by a thud, made everyone turn around and look at the window.

A high pitched voice, belonging to a man, cried:

"Hang tight. I shan't be a tick!"

Then a wiry gentleman, whose age was difficult to determine, shuffled from behind a half finished pyramid of books smoothing his clothes and hair. He wore a tight black shirt with drainpipe trousers and silver shoes which pointed at the toe. His grey and peroxide blonde hair was expertly sculpted into a quiff. He smiled and gave a regal nod to customers as he glided towards the counter artfully disguising a twisted ankle.

"Miss Drake!"

The man paused before Esme and gracefully unfurled an arm like he was presenting himself in a ballroom. He waltzed behind the counter, and did a little turn before placing his fingers on its surface.

"And how are we this fine morning? And your father, Professor Drake? I haven't seen him in here for quite some time. I trust he is keeping well?"

Mr Featherstone the shop keeper was a polite and gentle soul whose admiration for Esme's father was about as well a kept secret as his clumsiness.

"Yes very well thank you, Mr Featherstone. Keeping busy as usual," replied Esme pleasantly, placing the book in front of him. On spotting her choice, Mr Featherstone's face lit up. He lifted it and sniffed the pages with a face so enraptured it might have been a bottle of frankincense.

"Ahh a classic if there ever was one," he gushed.

"And an undisputed favourite of mine. Now is it a gift? Would you like me to wrap it for you?"

Esme was fairly certain gift wrapping wasn't part of the service at Blackwells. Though Mr Featherstone would happily add an extra flourish for his favoured customers.

"That's very kind Mr Featherstone. But this one's actually for me. I thought it might be nice to read it on the lawn in Hertford, since the weather's good."

"Why, that sounds perfect, what a fine plan," Mr Featherstone proclaimed, with a slight tweak of his quiff at the mention of excellence.

"The very birthplace of the tale, the fountain from which its creator drew sustenance. Learning all that is fine about this great city and the wisdom which lies between its walls."

Then, slipping the book into a bag and handing it delicately to Esme, he added.

"Oh that reminds me dear. I believe you left something behind when you were last in our reading room."

Esme didn't have a chance to protest before Mr Featherstone vanished beneath the counter. She heard scuffles, mumbles and "I'm sure it's in here somewhere", followed by a loud clunk which she assumed was his head. Then he appeared calm faced, smoothing his perfect hair with one hand, while holding a teddy bear in the other. Confused and mildly offended, Esme started shaking her head:

"Oh no that's definitely not…"

"You see I found it when you were in here a couple of weeks ago," Mr Featherstone interjected.

"Right by that chair you were sitting in over there," he said, waggling a long, thin finger towards the reading area.

"And I wasn't totally sure that it was yours until I saw the name on the tag… see?" he said, turning over a cream label tied around the bear's neck with a red ribbon, so that she could read it clearly. Esme instantly felt the chills and fears of the night before washing over her again. There before her, in the same green italic writing as the cream envelopes, was her full name: "*Esmeralda.*

She reluctantly took the bear in both hands holding it away from her body like it was an alien species. It was an old, jointed bear, with pale sandy fur, worn down in patches from being loved. Its paws were covered in soft cream fabric with dark brown stitches for its claws, nose and mouth. And its head had furry ears and glass eyes with large black pupils. It was a handsome bear, she had to admit, but why was it left for her?

"Well I wish you well in your encounters with Mr Ryder and Mr Flyte," Mr Featherstone went on breezily, seemingly unaware of her discontent.

"Oh to be meeting those gentlemen for the very first time. How I envy you," he went on, before placing Esme's money carefully into the till, then ramming it shut with such force it made them both jump.

Esme's head was starting to spin, just like it had in the library, by the time she got to the exit. What with Hetty's card, the mysterious teddy bear, plus Mr Featherstone's erratic flamboyance, she felt a desperate need for air. She was about to walk out of the door and take a deep breath when the shadow of a man appeared, blocking her path.

"I'm so sorry," she mumbled, looking up to see who was standing in her way. Then she felt the blood flow to her cheeks as she saw the face of a man she had only recently become familiar with, but couldn't get out of her mind. Rafferty Montgomery was standing in the doorway, in a burgundy and gold striped rugby kit, looking straight back at her. Then she saw his sparkling blue eyes move down to her hand, still holding the bear, and his mouth twist into an amused grin. She felt her face flush again.

"Oh no this isn't…"

For the second time that morning she attempted to deny possession of the
unsolicited bear. Rafferty, grinning in a way that both infuriated and humiliated her, calmly stood back and said:

"After you."

Then she squeezed past, stuffing the bear in her satchel, before turning right and storming off in the direction of the Bridge of Sighs.

Of all the times to run into Rafferty Montgomery, why did she have to be holding a teddy like a child? And it wasn't even her teddy! Why on earth would someone have left it for her? And who did he think he was smirking at her! She was starting to feel like the whole world was playing a game at her expense. Like some in-joke amongst the adults, she wasn't old enough to share.

Esme was still fuming by the time she turned into the entrance to Hertford College. The porter, a friend of her father's, gave her a nod as she passed the lodge, to let her know it was ok to go in. The orderly sight of the college's manicured lawn in its charming quad went some way to soothing her nerves. Not only did Brideshead Revisited's author, Evelyn Waugh, study at Hertford, it was also one of Esme's favourites. She loved the turret with diagonal windows which appeared to twist around its spiral staircase, and the fact the Bridge of Sighs connected its two halves.

Finding a quiet space, Esme sat and pulled the book out of her bag. Part of her resented being manipulated into carrying on with this charade. But with a head too inquisitive not to find out more and since reading was the best way to ease her mind, she took a breath and turned the first page. Within minutes she had been transported back to the city she knew so well but during the decadent 1920s. An Oxford student called Charles Ryder, a young painter like herself, was getting caught in the world of a charismatic aristocrat called Sebastian Flyte. Esme found herself exploring his family's lavish castle, with its opulent domed roof and extravagant fountain, becoming almost as enchanted as the protagonist. She found Sebastian's delightful eccentricities, particularly his fondness for Aloysius his teddy bear, as bonkers as they were endearing. Until his quirks rapidly descended into chaos and he started drinking heavily and getting into trouble. Had this book been sent her way as a warning Esme wondered, since she was also bridging the gap between youth and adulthood?

At lunchtime she wandered to The Kings Arms, a large old pub painted a dusky pink, on the corner where Broad Street meets New College Lane. She bought a tuna baguette, a bowl of chips and a soda and lime then took them to a picnic table by the road in the sun. She saw Rupert sweep past on his bike in the direction of the Natural History Museum and smiled and waved the book at him. He beamed back shouting "Bravo!" before cycling on, his chequered legs moving even faster than the day before. Then after lunch, she took the book back to Hertford, and read on.

Around six o'clock, once relations had soured between Charles and the Flytes, and he'd become an unhappily married yet successful painter, Esme remembered she'd promised to meet her father at Teddy Hall. She squeezed the book alongside the unwanted teddy bear in her bag, then wandered down the narrow and winding New College Lane. She smiled at Mr Frogmore, who was gloomily sorting post in the lodge, then made her way to the little round well in the middle of the quad.

There was something about this solid ring of mediaeval stone, delicately mottled from centuries of lichen, which felt like a portal to the centre of the earth. Esme loved to imagine the ancient monks who studied here, drawing their water in ages gone by, as far back as the thirteenth century. She ran her hand around a Latin inscription, gilded inside, reading: "With joy you will draw water from the wells of salvation," and felt the weight of its significance. Then she perched on its edge, just as she used to when waiting for her father as a child, and continued to read her book.

The quad was quiet and empty apart from a couple of sparrows on the lawn, and she could see the light on in her father's study. It was the end of the day and her eyelids were starting to flicker, as she came to the final chapters of her book. Sebastian had now fallen sick in a Moroccan monastery, while Charles was "homeless, childless, middle-aged and loveless". As the characters' fortunes continued to worsen, Esme felt herself becoming increasingly weary. Her legs were sore from running after Rupert, and her satchel had started to feel surprisingly heavy. Wanting rid of it and its unwanted bear, she tried to swing the strap over her neck, but felt a counter tension fighting against her. "How strange," she mumbled, feeling confused and irritable. With her shoulder becoming sore she tried again, but felt a stronger pull, like a magnet drawing her back. It felt as if the bag was getting heavier and heavier, like a balloon filling with water. Until her body simply couldn't fight it any more.

In a flash she fell back, everything went black and she was falling, falling, falling into the depths of the well. Filled with terror, she felt her body twisting and turning, grasping at air and dreading the inevitable. She was screaming but couldn't hear her voice, just the sound of blood pumping in her ears. And then a light started flickering behind her eyelids, like a movie reel, getting faster and faster, until faint images started forming in her mind:.

Summer mouthing: "Drink!"

Rupert saying: "Hurry!"

And a grand and enigmatic Dougal whispering: "Magic!"

Then everything flashed bright white, like the inside of The Glink, and the falling suddenly stopped.

## Chapter 12 - A Game of Chess

Esme felt sick and disorientated from spinning around and her stomach was aching from the drop. She was breathing heavily, with her eyes squeezed shut, too terrified to open them. Her mouth felt dry from screaming and had a bitter and metallic taste. Still lying down she cautiously scraped her fingers across the ground, and felt a surprisingly smooth texture. Then she nervously blinked her eyes open, and eased herself up to a seated position. Around her was a perfectly round white room, about the breadth of her arm span, with a white velvet cushion filling the base. She looked up, hoping to see light at the top of the well, but was met by a solid domed ceiling. There were no windows, and the room was completely empty, apart from the teddy which had fallen from her bag. Struggling to catch her breath, now feeling claustrophobic, she started pressing and thumping against the walls, her cries deadened by the curvature of the walls. Until a small doorway silently opened up before her. Quickly grabbing the teddy, she crouched down and carefully climbed through.

Esme stood up straight and heard the door slam shut behind her. She spun around to see if it was still there, but all she found was a large bookcase. It didn't budge even though she pushed and kicked it. She felt her palms go clammy and her heart racing, and turned back, afraid of who or what she might find. But she was all alone, standing in an elegant dining room.

The walls were papered in a delicate sage green damask with a dining table covered in lace and silverware laid between. An ornate ceiling with gold leaf detail soared above with crystals falling like tear drops from a chandelier. Full length sash windows draped with plush golden curtains stood at one end with an inlaid drinks cabinet at the other. And two fat cherubs were sculpted into a marble fireplace supporting a large mirror framed in gold. The place felt stately yet strangely familiar. Could this be the Brideshead Castle she'd been reading about, Esme wondered?

She placed the teddy in a carved dining chair then quickly headed towards a door at the far end of the room. But before her hand reached the brass door knob it flew open, leaving Esme pinned against the wall, trying to control her breath so as not to be heard. Then, to her surprise, she heard a little girl's voice:

"There you are Aloysius! I've been looking for you everywhere. Now come along, Annabel's been waiting for us."

Esme cautiously peered out to see who the tiny voice belonged to:

"And you Elizabeth. Hurry up," the child continued brightly, spotting her immediately. She was about eight years old, dressed in brown dungarees and a pink floral blouse with her hair curled up tightly in rags.

"We're going to play chess," she went on happily, before skipping out of the door swinging the bear upside down by its leg. *Annabel and Elizabeth*, Esme thought to herself. Neither were names she remembered from Brideshead. She quickly followed the girl into an imposing hallway with marble pillars and a sweeping staircase at its heart. A pale pink door gave it a country manor feel along with darkened oil paintings of horses and pastoral scenes. The soft scent of roses from French urns was reassuringly familiar while the irregular tick of a grandfather clock welcomed her home. Because this was part of the house

Esme immediately recognised, although she hadn't been here for many years, and couldn't imagine why she'd ended up here. This was her grandparents' house: Avaley Hall.

The child was already at the top of the stairs beckoning impatiently.

"Come quick! There won't be much time before mother calls," she cried, before vanishing behind a swirling wrought iron bannister. Esme climbed the stairs towards a vast mirror at the centre of a spacious landing lined with wall lamps and many doors. She followed the little girl to the left and found her waiting in a large nursery filled with sunlight. Esme remembered this room too, but not quite like this. The bed was in its place near the door but this one was larger with four wooden posts and cotton sheets embroidered with flowers. Esme's handsome rocking horse from their house in Summertown was between two windows where she remembered a writing desk used to be. There was a rug made up of coloured rags spread across polished floorboards, scattered with toys. And four pink cushions were placed around a chess board balanced on an upturned vegetable crate, with chess pieces lined up around all four sides. The girl was sitting cross legged on one cushion with the teddy bear perched opposite.

"Come sit Elizabeth," she said, patting the cushion to her right with her small outstretched hand.

"The rest of us are ready to play."

Esme looked around to see if anyone else was there. Seeing no one, she sat down.

"So since Annabel was kept waiting, it seems only fair that she should go first," the little girl went on matter of factly, shooting a disapproving look in Esme's direction. Then she picked up a castle from the side where there was an empty space and placed it in the middle of the board.

"What a perfect way to start the game Annabel!" the little girl gushed, clasping her hands together in delight and looking approvingly at her invisible friend.

"The castle means all the others will have somewhere to live," she went on knowingly, glancing at Esme to check she was following. Esme, not sure she was, simply smiled and nodded back. Then the girl picked up a Queen from the bear's side of the board, and placed it next to the castle in the centre.

"And that's another fine move by Aloysius. Now the castle has a Queen, we will have somebody to rule the castle," she went on cheerfully. Then she picked up a knight from her own side of the board and placed it alongside the other pieces.

"And of course the Queen will need a horse, in order to travel to all the other kingdoms in the land," she went on, before gazing up expectantly at Esme. Esme, thinking she was following the rules, picked up a King, but seeing the little girl's horrified face promptly put it down again. She hesitated, then picked up a bishop and placed it with the others.

"And now we have a bishop, the Queen can go to Church…?" she offered cautiously, hoping the girl would approve. To which the child simply smiled and rocked happily from side to side holding the edges of her cushion. Then she started again from the empty side of the board.

After Esme had completed a couple more rounds, making a particularly good impression by adding a pawn as "the Queen's magic elf", she finally felt it was safe to ask a question:

"So I heard you call your bear Aloysius. Why did you name him that?"

"I didn't silly!" the girl replied brusquely, her eyes wide with astonishment.

"It was Daddy's bear. You know that. Aloysius. 'The perfect name for the bear of a child with a big imagination'. Perhaps I'll understand when I'm a bit older, Daddy said. But then grown ups are always saying that aren't they. They think us children don't understand anything. When in fact it's perfectly obvious. Because I've never met anyone else with a name like Aloysius have you? Which means Daddy must have made it up. Just like I made up this game."

Esme, thoroughly enjoying this little girl's way of thinking, nodded approvingly and carried on listening.

"And it's not like Daddy knows everything. Because he says when I grow up I'll be presented at debutante balls and will probably marry a duke or a prince. But I think that sounds ab-so-lute-ly horr-end-ous!" the little girl moaned, emphasising each of the syllables with such contempt it made Esme burst out laughing.

"Because when I grow up I'm going to be a scientist, and then I'll be able to learn everything there is to know about plants and animals. And then once I've learnt all of that I'm going to be an author, and write books about all of the adventures I've had travelling the world, discovering hundreds of new flowers."

On hearing this, Esme immediately understood why the Queen ruled the Kingdom and the King didn't get to play in the castle in the little girl's game of chess. It made her warm to her and her refreshing outlook on life even more. Then just as the girl was about to pick up another chess piece, a woman's voice called out from another room:

"Oh Sienna. Come here now please darling. If we leave your hair much longer you'll end up curled up as tight as a poodle!"

Which made the little girl put both hands across her mouth and let out a high pitched giggle. Then she picked up the bear and skipped happily out of the room, calling:

"Come on Annabel, come on Elizabeth. Mummy needs to do your hair too!"

"Sienna??"

Esme stood up slowly, trying to digest what the woman had said and who the little girl must be, before hurrying out in case she should lose her. She spotted another door open on the landing with bright sunlight pouring through onto the carpet. She instinctively followed the sunbeams and walked in. The large bed from the nursery now appeared to be in this room, with its posts painted white and a small bouquet of white roses, lily of the valley and gypsophila placed on a cream satin bedspread. There was a Provence style dressing table in front of the bed between sash windows overlooking a garden rich in twisting topiary and mossy statues. And an oval looking glass stood in the corner of the room with a soft cream rug at its base. A woman in a long silk ivory gown, which hung low down her back
was standing in front of the mirror, with an older lady, in a smart mauve dress and jacket just above the knee, combing her hair. Her long auburn hair. This was Esme's mother and grandmother: Sienna and Priscilla Blythe.

Esme was now sitting on the end of the bed watching, but neither woman appeared to notice her. She saw her grandmother pick up a mother of pearl comb attached to a long chiffon veil, trimmed with lace, and fix it to the back of her daughter's head. And then the pair kissed one another lightly on the cheek. She heard a soft knock on the door and her grandfather Michael walked in, wearing a navy suit with a white rose buttonhole, carrying a gift. It was flat, wrapped in silver paper with a fine ribbon tied in a bow. He handed it to Sienna. Esme watched her mother unwrap it and pull out a cream hardback book. Its cover was slightly yellowing and worn around the edges with a faded grey crest swirling around a crimson title on the front. She turned the front page and gasped.

"I can't believe he remembered," she said, gazing up at her parents.

"It's a first edition of Brideshead Revisited. I told him it was my favourite book years ago, when we first met and used to walk around the deer park. Can you remember how I waited for years to find out why your teddy bear was called Aloysius Daddy? Before you finally handed me the book?"

Michael nodded, smiling adoringly at his daughter.

"And then it was love at first sight. Just as it was for me with you and your mother," he replied, his voice just as solid and warm as Esme remembered.

"And now it would seem I am obliged to share some of that love with another fine gentleman," he added, offering his arm to Sienna.

"Shall we?"

Esme watched as Michael and Sienna left the room with Priscilla, who was still fixing a pin to her oversized hat, following closely behind. With her head in a spin over what she'd just witnessed, she ran onto the landing, watching as the three of them drifted down the staircase. The front door was now wide open with bright sunshine pouring onto a parquet floor. Esme watched her mother and grandparents walk between the French urns filled with white roses flanking the stairs then step into the bright light. She felt an uneasiness in the pit of her stomach she couldn't explain. As the tip of the veil swept past the bottom stair she started making her way down, as the group walked towards the door. Then she watched them vanish into the light and knew exactly what that feeling was. Because it was the same feeling she'd had the day she found out her Mum had gone missing when she was a little girl.

Feeling her panic rising she hurried her step, hoping she could catch her. The light was getting brighter reaching further across the hall. Then it touched the bottom stair which instantly vanished, and started climbing up the stairs, melting them one by one. Terrified, Esme turned around and tried to run back to the top. But it was too late. In a flash, the step beneath her feet had gone too. And she was falling, falling, falling once again.

# Chapter 13 - A Grasshopper

Esme's body was pouring with sweat and her arms and legs were trembling from the fall. She found herself lying on a firm surface, her eyes tight shut feeling hot and constricted. Desperate to break free, she pushed away the mass weighing her down. Then, feeling cool air against her skin, she hesitantly opened her eyes. Her vision was blurry but she couldn't mistake what was directly above her. Because it was the same night sky, painted onto her ceiling, that she woke up to every morning.

Confused and flustered she kicked the covers off and sat up in bed. She was still fully clothed but her satchel was hanging from her door and the old teddy bear, or Aloysius as her mother had called him, was on her bed between Eddie and Violet. She rubbed her eyes wondering if she was still dreaming. And if it had all been a dream, how and when did she get back to the barge? Shaken and bewildered, she swung her legs out of bed and shuffled over the rug to her satchel. She opened it to find Brideshead Revisited still in there. She still had the sensation of falling in her body with visions of chess pieces, open books and wedding veils spinning around her head.

Feeling more exhausted than she had the previous morning, Esme looked at the gold watch which was still on her wrist. It was already 8am. She quickly ran to the tiny bathroom on the barge before dashing back to her room and pulling on her school uniform: a bottle green blazer and skirt embroidered with a gold crest of an eagle and a lion, with a white shirt and golden tie. Then, rushing into the heart of the barge, she stopped dead in her tracks. On the table was a small book covered in illustrations of rabbits, birds, flowers and butterflies with a pink post-it note saying "Good luck!" She'd asked her Dad to bring the collection of nature poems home for her a couple of days ago. And today was the day she was due to recite one of them in front of the entire school.

Just as her panic was rising she heard a door at the other end of the barge creak open.

"Ahhh thank goodness. There you are Petal!"

Andrew Drake was walking barefoot towards the kitchen, in blue striped pyjamas, with his mousey hair ruffled.

"Was beginning to think you'd fallen down the well!"

But Esme was barely listening. Pulling Brideshead from her satchel and replacing it with the book she wished she'd been reading, she called out:

"Sorry Dad! Late for school."

Before speeding out of the barge, leaving Andrew blinking without his spectacles, calling:

"Well at least I know you're in one piece! Did you get the poems…?"

But Esme was already hurtling down the river towards Folly Bridge and the nearby bus stop.

Elegant wrought iron gates adorned with an eagle and lion usually gave Esme a thrill of gratitude as she entered Elm Tree Academy. Her grandparents had left just enough money in their wills to cover her education and she silently thanked them everyday. The circular lawn, surrounded by a broad pathway lined with elm trees, was extremely welcoming, as were the soft sandstone steps up to its arched wooden doors. But gazing up at the words engraved above them this morning made her stomach feel like it was falling down the well again. "In Omnia Paratus", Latin for "Always be Prepared" was the school motto, and one Esme imagined could soon come back to haunt her.

Reluctantly, she dragged her shiny black shoes up the steps, and joined the other pupils filing down a red brick corridor. Triumphant sports teams beamed down on her from glass cabinets filled with sparkling trophies on either side, their success a harsh reminder that practice and hard work pay off.

"How could I have forgotten about this?" Esme muttered to herself, keeping her head down lest the smugness of the athletes' photos should throw her even further off kilter. She was the kind of person who would revise for weeks on end before exams and always gave her homework in on time. Forgetting to learn a poem, when her error would be made so public, was extremely out of character and rather worrying she thought.

Just as she was bracing herself to enter the school's vast assembly hall and face the music, an unmistakable voice stopped her in her tracks.

"Brains!!!"

A pair of green blazored arms were wrapped tightly around her neck from behind, and a distinctive blonde plait with a bow on the end was hanging over her shoulder.

"I'm so glad I caught you!" Summer went on breathlessly.

"I was up half the night trying to decide between Ode to a Nightingale by Keats and To a Skylark by Shelley. There are just so many fabulous poems about nature it's impossible to decide. So I've narrowed it down to birds, you know, as a nice gesture to Aristotle. But now I'm flip flopping between my two favourites, which is a bit of a bum. So I thought since you've got the poetry brains, Brains, perhaps you could decide?"

They were now half way down the hall, which was already packed, and the sight of a tall stage with thick green curtains bearing down on them was making Esme's legs feel wobbly. Summer now had her arm linked through hers and was staring at her intently. Esme didn't have chance to respond before she went on:

"Although Ode to a Nightingale is a classic, I'm wondering whether it might be better to go with something a bit more off-piste. You know? I always hate to be predictable. But then To a Skylark is terribly long, so perhaps it would be better to just stick with Keats after all. Yes, I think that's what I'll do. Oh I don't know!"

Esme could see her headmistress Miss Gilbert standing behind a wooden lectern, with jet black hair scraped into a bun and half moon glasses on an elongated nose. She wore a bulky brown jacket, made of the kind of wool that made Esme feel itchy, with a matching skirt to her calves. Esme felt her beady eyes follow her as she walked in front of the stage then up the steps to join the other pupils waiting in the wings. She already felt judged.

"Oh and I never asked you," Summer was attempting but failing to whisper.

"Which poem are you doing?"

Esme had used the twenty minute bus ride to memorise Mary Oliver's The Summer Day. But most of it had now been replaced by the words of another Summer.

"Still deciding too if I'm honest," she replied vaguely, fiddling with her hair. She was hoping she might be able to remember an old classic if her chosen poem should evade her.

"But why don't you stick with Keats. I know everyone always enjoys a bit of Keats."

Summer squeezed Esme's arm tight and beamed at her appreciatively, before the thunderous voice of their headmistress made them straighten up and smooth their blazers, readying themselves for action.

"Good Morning Elm Tree Academy!"

Miss Gilbert's voice was heavy and commanding. She was clutching the sides of the lectern with jagged fingers and scanning the room like a hawk.

"I trust that you all had a pleasant May Bank Holiday, and are back rested and fully prepared for the difficult work ahead of you."

She managed to roll her r's in a way that made her words sound like both an accusation and a threat. She paused briefly to push her spectacles back up her nose before adopting a slightly more cordial tone:

"Now as you know we are seriously committed to the environment here at Elm Tree Academy. Which is why I have chosen the theme of nature for our monthly poetry recital. This morning we will be listening to verses by our Sixth Form students. So without further ado please welcome Freya Farnham onto the stage."

Applause broke out as Miss Gilbert swept her arm like a huge wing, to present a petite girl with a shiny chestnut bob, onto the stage. Finding herself dwarfed by the lectern she walked assuredly to the centre instead. Summer and Esme glanced at one another uneasily as she paused and sniffed the air, taking in the audience with complete self confidence. Before theatrically closing her eyes and announcing, in a voice disarmingly loud for such a tiny person, that she'd be reciting I Wandered Lonely as a Cloud by Wordsworth. Which made Summer tut and pretend to yawn and Esme stifle a giggle.

After a word perfect rendition Freya delivered the final line: "And dances with the daffodils!" with an elaborate courtesy, adding several more as applause broke out, like a ballerina taking an encore. Then she tiptoed back into the wings with similar grace, which made Summer pretend to vomit into the curtain. Miss Gilbert appeared back at the lectern, so spontaneously it seemed like magic, with a face entirely unmoved.

"And next... we have Esmeralda Drake," she announced coldy, with her eyes hungrily searching the wings and a Dracula-like swish of her arm. Miss Gilbert had never hidden the fact she found Esme's imagination too fanciful and her passion for books over indulgent. Her austere nature alone made Esme feel like she was being set up to fail. She glanced nervously at Summer, who was now giving her an enthusiastic thumbs up and ushering her towards the stage. For a split second Esme considered cutting her losses and making a run for it. But, with her teacher's icy gaze still upon her, she lowered her head and marched towards her fate. Below her were faces of around two hundred students, blinking up with eager expectation. She looked behind them and saw the school's towering pipe organ on a large balcony. Its organist, tiny by comparison, was waiting patiently too. Wishing she could just click her fingers and disappear, Esme solemnly took her place behind the lecturn:

"The Summer Day - by Mary Oliver."

She introduced the poem slowly and clearly, before taking a deep breath to calm her mind.

"Who made the world?
Who made the swan, and the black bear?
Who made the grasshopper?
This grasshopper I mean,
The one who has flung herself out of the grass,
The one who…"

Esme paused and cleared her throat, trying to visualise the words on the page.

"The one who has… I mean the one who was… Sorry!"

She shook her head and tried again. But now all she could see in the audience was her mother's face as a little girl, gazing up at her from her chess board. Standing here trying to remember a poem about a grasshopper now felt utterly absurd, when there were so many more important mysteries to be solved. Sensing her head teacher twitching with anticipation, she cleared her throat, ready to try again. Or perhaps she should change tack and go for something else, like Shakespeare's 'Shall I Compare thee to a Summer's Day'? But it was no use. Esme's head was spinning again with images of envelopes, books and teddy bears. Then before she knew it she was racing off the stage and back into the wings.

"Brains! What the hell was that?" Summer hissed, before hearing her name, smoothing her pigtails, and gliding onto the stage. Esme's head was now so full of noise she didn't even hear her friend's recital, let alone know which poem she'd opted for. What the hell *was* she doing? Since turning sixteen so many things had changed. Not only did she not know what she was doing, she really wasn't sure who was anymore. In what felt like a matter of seconds there was another round of applause, before Miss Gilbert barked something inaudible and the pipe organ broke into the rousing first bars of All Things Bright and Beautiful. Esme felt nauseous, but Summer was now back in the wings, dragging her out of a side exit by her hand. Until she was standing outside in a cobbled quad, gasping for air, with her friend gently rubbing her back.

Esme had no idea how she made it through the first lessons of the day. French wasn't her strongest subject and she had failed to inherit her mother's talent for Music. She sat at the back of both classes, solemn and subdued, until the sound of a bell finally liberated her. Minutes later she was surrounded by a cacophony of knives, forks and noisy chatter along with the concerned faces of Priya, Summer and Freddy. They were sitting at a long dining table in an old red brick room, beneath dozens of stained glass windows painted with trees. Golden crests of an eagle and lion stood at each end, with the school's warning to be prepared, *In Omnia Paratus*, looming down on Esme like a stiff rebuke.

"It all just went clear out of my head," she said wearily, searching her friends' faces for comfort, feeling utterly mortified.

"One minute I was talking about the grasshopper. The next, all I could think about was…"

She paused, unsure of whether to go on. Seeing her friends' earnest faces, she lowered her head and softly added:

"My Mum."

"Oh babe," Priya cried, rubbing her hand, her eyes wide with empathy.

"You see I've been getting these peculiar notes," Esme went on.

"Well they're cards really. They've got quotes from Brideshead Revisited on them. Which led me to Blackwells to buy the book, where Mr Featherstone gave me a teddy bear."

Freddy clicked his fingers around his head three times before holding up his palm and saying:

"Hold up a hot second. A bear? From a book shop?"

"Yeah," Esme went on.

"Because he thought it was mine. The cards and the bear all had the same writing on them, spelling out Esmeralda, you see."

"So some creep is sending you all this crazy stuff?" Summer asked, sounding thoroughly incensed, but relishing the drama.

"Hire an investigator!" she went on.

"No I mean it. Sounds to me like you've got yourself a stalker. I've read all about this kind of thing in those women's magazines my Mum loves. You have to nip it in the bud now. Before things really start to escalate."

"The thing is," Esme went on slowly.

"Then I had a dream about Mum."

She watched Summer's demeanour subtly brighten. She'd found a book about dreams in her parents' study and been obsessed with them ever since.

"You see I was reading Brideshead Revisited in Teddy Hall, but then I was falling down the well. I found a doorway to my grandparents' house, then met my Mum as a little girl, before seeing her on her wedding morning."

All three friends had lowered their cutlery and were leaning in, listening intently.

"Sounds pretty trippy," said Priya, looking towards Freddy who was nodding in agreement.

"Hmmm. I know exactly what's going on here," Summer added like a pseudo detective.

"Go on…" Esme responded, eager for her analysis.

"Well it's obvious," Summer said bluntly.

"You're having a midlife crisis."

"I'm having a what?"

Esme almost spat out her orange juice.

"But I'm only 16!"

"Well a quarter life crisis then, or would it be a sixth? Oh I don't know," Summer went on, a little irked to be hampered by details.

"Look. It's obvious that your birthday has triggered some sort of meltdown. Nothing at all to worry about. You've just gone a bit bonkers that's all," she went on, as if that ought to placate everyone.

"Okay…" Esme replied.

"So you're telling me the dream was a 'sixth life crisis', or possibly a nervous breakdown of sorts?"

"Exactly!" said Summer.

"A dream about falling is a classic sign of anxiety. You feel like you're losing control. It's like you thought you knew who you were yesterday, or before your big birthday, but now you're really not quite sure."

Esme nodded. That was how she'd been feeling. So much had happened lately it had changed the way she felt about just about everything.

"Oh and by the way. Your Mum wasn't really your Mum in the dream either," Summer went on, enjoying her own evaluation.

"She wasn't?" Esme asked, now starting to lose the thread again.

"Well who was she then?"

"Well she was *you* silly! You're having an identity crisis, on account of your birthday and a lack of a strong female role model. Apart from Bambi and I of course. Which means part of you wants to go back to being a child, while the other is in a rush to grow up."

"I see," said Esme. She had to admit Summer's explanation did make some sense. Although she felt a little bit disappointed that she hadn't really met her Mum.

"But then what about the book?" she asked.

"What book?" Summer said, looking puzzled.

"The Brideshead Revisited book. In my dream it got delivered to my Mum as a gift from my Dad on their wedding morning."

"Well that's easy too," Summer went on, stretching her arms back to show how simple this all was.

"It's just another classic sign of stress. You've been getting all these weird cards with stuff from the book. Which means you're now having whacky dreams about it, and your inner child is crying out for your parents to protect you. Books represent a desire for information and knowledge you see. So it's basically your subconscious trying to work it all out. Helping you get a grip!"

"Oooh she's very good isn't she?" Freddy crooned fawningly, hanging off Summer's every word. Then he pointed at all their empty dinner plates, clicking his fingers to get their attention.

"Right you crazy cats," he said.

"That's quite enough psychoanalysis for one day. I'd say we're in serious need of something to lighten the mood. Snap this one out of her post birthday blues. Round of croquet?"

Priya and Summer jumped up crying "Oooh yes, let's!" swinging their school bags over their shoulders then striding off between the rows of tables. Esme felt too drained to follow. She cocked her head towards Freddy and whispered:

"Do you actually know the rules to croquet Fred?"

Freddy smoothed his hair back, smiled serenely and chimed:

"No, I haven't the faintest clue," before sweeping out of the dining room, leaving Esme sluggishly trailing behind.

## Chapter 14 - The Lotus Flower

Half an hour later, in a peaceful corner of the school's leafy grounds, only Summer and Freddy were left playing the game. Summer had carefully laid iron hoops around a small garden lined with neat box hedges, selecting the blue and black balls for herself and Priya, leaving the red and yellow ones for Esme and Freddy. Then they'd taken turns hitting them through the hoops with long wooden mallets, with Freddy making up his own rules to infuriate Summer, until she'd finally thrown down her mallet in frustration. At this point Esme subtly backed out, wandering across the lawn to rest beneath a lofty elm tree.

Feeling the sturdy bark against her back and sunrays piercing and flickering through the leaves, made her feel safe and nourished. Until another flashback would throw her mind into turmoil, making her wrap her arms around her legs and bury her head in her knees. Sensing her torment, Priya placed her mallet back in the old English willow basket it came from and walked quietly over. She gently slid down the trunk of the elm, before resting her head on her friend's shoulder.

"It's tough isn't it...?" she said softly, gazing at the pair still playing croquet beneath the old red turrets and sandstone bay windows of the school. Esme heard her friend's mellow voice over the sound of the breeze through the leaves and felt immediately soothed.

"This life I mean," Priya went on.

"When just yesterday it was almost as simple as the grasshopper's," she added with a wry grin, hoping to lighten the mood.

Esme smiled faintly, hearing the clunk of a mallet meeting a ball, and the words of the poem now flooding back all too late.

"Snapping her wings open and floating away," she replied dreamily, following a leaf gently drifting down from above until it landed on the grass.

"But now nothing seems the way it was," Esme added.

"There's just so much confusion, so many questions. I mean how are we possibly supposed to know what to do with this 'one wild and precious life'?"

"But that's just it," Priya replied calmly, recognizing the final words of the poem.

"Don't you see? You knew the words to the poem all along. You were just trying too hard to find them."

Esme stretched her legs out on the grass and let out a deep sigh. Priya was always so good at reading people. What she said made total sense. She *was* in a rush to have everything worked out to get to the next stage of her life. Making little time for the present at all.

"You see you have always been so logical," Priya went on.

"Trying to make sense of everything, constantly searching for meanings. When there's often little reason to things anyway. It's like looking up into this tree. Trying so hard to make out the solid branches, that you almost miss the beauty and complexity of the leaves."

Esme gazed upwards and saw a vibrant cluster of green, gently moving beneath a deep blue sky. It immediately made her feel calm. How could one possibly be afraid of the future, when there was so much wonder in the world yet to be discovered? But then, just as she was starting to relax, another memory made her shudder.

"Priya," she said slowly, raising herself up and turning towards her.

"You know how to read Tarot cards don't you?"

"Yes of course," she replied, pulling herself up too.

"I always thought that kind of thing didn't interest you."

"Well it doesn't really. Or it didn't," Esme went on, not sure how best to explain herself.

"It's just that I received another card. But this one was different."

"A tarot card?" Priya asked, her eyes widening.

"Yes. But it was the death tarot card! It was attached to the front of the barge over a bunch of dead roses," Esme went on, getting chills again at the memory.

"And I'm pretty sure I know who sent this one. Do you know that old lady who lives on that strange barge, Asphodel?"

"Hetty," Priya replied instantly.

"Didn't she used to perform as a mermaid in the seventies? I've heard all sorts of stories about her wearing a shimmering tail, swimming around pools of the rich and the famous at cocktail parties."

"Nothing would surprise me," said Esme absentmindedly. There were so many stories about Hetty it was hard to know which were true and which were local folklore.

"Anyway… I'd had a run in with her earlier in the day. She wanted to read my cards but I was in a hurry. Then later that evening…"

"You found the card…" added Priya.

"Exactly," said Esme, staring at her friend, hoping she could help her see sense again.

"Okaaay," she replied.

"Well that is a little creepy. The fact that she did that I mean. But the card itself is nothing to worry about. In fact in many ways it's a good thing. You see the death card doesn't actually mean death. It's all about transformation and change. Letting go of the old to make way for the future. Pretty much exactly all the things you've been experiencing lately," she continued steadily, watching Esme visibly soften with relief.

"I see," she replied.

"There I go again. Trying so hard to work out the facts that I miss the real meaning altogether."

Priya said nothing. Just smiled knowingly at her friend.

"However," Esme went on, getting serious again.

"There was something else. When I turned it over there was a warning, written in red ink across the back. It said 'Beware the Dark Stranger'!"

Priya threw her head back and burst into a fit of giggles.

"I'm sorry! I really shouldn't laugh," she said, leaning forward and shaking her hair over her face, then smoothing it back behind her ears and trying to compose herself.

"But you'd think someone supposedly in tune with the spiritual world could have come up with something more original than that. It's like something from an Agatha Christie novel! But again, I really wouldn't worry. It sounds like she's just trying to wind you up. I mean at the end of the day we're all strangers to begin with aren't we really? Until we get to know one another."

"I guess," said Esme, still confused by it all but feeling a little more reassured. They sat in silence for a moment, watching Summer doing a cartwheel and Freddy hitting a croquet ball like he was playing golf, before shouting "Sorry!" at a group of girls walking down a nearby path.

"I mean look at that pair," Priya said with a grin, pointing at Freddy who was now strutting around his mallet like he was dancing with a cane, making Summer shriek with laughter.

"Now they don't waste their time reading into things too deeply do they? They just get on with it. We're here for a good time, not a long time!"

"Absolute pair of nutters," Esme said lovingly, watching Freddy now dancing the Charleston and feeling grateful to have such fabulous friends. Then she caught Priya studying her.

"Oh babe. You do look tired," she said kindly, rubbing her arm gently.

"Look I know you've had a lot going on lately. And that it's brought a lot of stuff up. Particularly about… your Mum. But it's these difficult times that make us stronger. It's how we grow."

Then gracefully shifting position, so one leg was bent in front of the other, with her palms outstretched on her knees, she went on:

"Look. Just think of yourself like the lotus flower. It grows beneath the water's surface, amongst the dirt and mud. But it's that very chaos that helps it eventually become so strong and beautiful."

The breeze was gently blowing her hair back with the sunlight making her features glow. Her palms had moved into a prayer position, and were slowly raising up towards the sky.

"And then the rain simply slides off its petals until it gently opens up to the sunshine that follows."

With this she reached up and parted her hands, gracefully floating them down to her sides, palms up like a flower.

"It's all about inner growth and remembering who you are," she went on smoothly, placing her hands softly in her lap.

"But that's the thing," Esme replied, pulling her knees up and wrapping her arms around them protectively, wishing she had an ounce of Priya's self awareness.

"I'm not sure I really know who I am!"

"Well you're a Goddess of the Forest aren't you?" Priya cried out jubilantly, which made Esme smile, then burst into laughter.

"We all are!"

At the sound of laughter Summer and Freddy dropped their mallets and came running towards them. Summer had pulled her hair out of plaits so it streamed behind her and Fred's shirt was unbuttoned with his tie hanging in a loose knot. Esme watched them thundering down the lawn as carefree as children.

"What's all this?" Fun without us?" Fred asked breathlessly, dropping his hand to his hip, pretending to give them attitude.

"Well at least somebody's managed to put a smile on that one's face," he added, twirling a finger in Esme's direction.

"Now all she needs is a haircut and a makeover and we might even be able to get her a boyfriend."

"Freed!" Esme moaned, glancing towards the ends of her hair, which she had to admit were getting rather long.

"Ooooh perhaps that'll be your dark stranger," gushed Priya, before seeing Summer's wide eyed face and mouthing 'I'll tell you later', giving her a wink.

"Right then Froodle," said Summer brightly, using her pet name for Freddy and pulling him by his sleeve.

"First one to the statue gets a bonus point!"

She tore back up the garden towards a haughty looking stone griffin holding a broken crest in the centre of the lawn, with Freddy chasing close behind yelling:

"Cheat!"

Then they picked up their mallets, walloping the balls as hard as they could, teasing one another mercifully every time they missed the hoops. Esme had always thought how alike that pair were. So full of confidence, without a care for what anyone else thought of them. How she wished she could be a little more like them. As if reading her thoughts, Priya suddenly rested her chin on her shoulder, gazing up at her, before extending her little finger.

"Birds of a feather?" she said softly.

Esme hadn't heard her say that since they were at primary school, when they were so close it was almost like they were the same person. Extending her own pinky finger and linking it through Priya's, she whispered back:

"Forever and ever."

Then they stayed in the shade of the elm tree, watching the others playing and bickering in equal measure, until the ringing of a bell summoned them back into the school.

## Chapter 15 - Roots

The sun had set on a balmy Friday evening, sending swirls of scarlet, violet and molten gold across the sky. Andrew was sitting on the roof of his barge gazing up through his telescope. His eyes were fixed on a full moon, burning orange with the remnants of the day.

"Not sure I've ever seen her look more radiant," he said serenely, soaking in its sublime beauty.

"They call it the Flower Moon, you know. The full moon in May. It's from the Old Farmer's Almanac. Named because of all the fresh blooms growing at the start of Spring."

Dougal was shuffling impatiently in the deckchair beside him.

"Well of course," he replied tersely.

"I'm hardly in need of the moon to tell me that. I've only got to look at all the extra work. Pruning buddleia, cutting back lavender. And that's before a whole load of alliums and delphiniums have popped up and got in my way. I for one won't be worshipping the Flower Moon with the hippies and the dropouts!"

"Now, now old boy. It's just a bit of fun," said Andrew, trying to hide his amusement at his friend's indignation. He'd known Dougal long enough to appreciate he was at his happiest when having a grumble. Plus he was always a little tetchy until

Andrew had sampled and approved of his choice of wine.

"Speaking of flowers," he went on brightly, spotting his daughter pulling herself onto the roof. Esme had rushed straight to her room after school, desperate to rid herself of her uniform, and throw on some comfy jeans. Andrew had noticed she'd been a little quiet and withdrawn lately and was hoping everything was ok.

"My goodness we're like ships that pass in the night these days!"

"Hi Dad, Hi Dougal," Esme said cheerfully, going over to her father and kissing him on the cheek before sitting down cross legged. There was a fold out camping table laid out before the men. A wine bottle and corkscrew had been placed on a wooden tray with crystal wine glasses and a plate of crackers, grapes and the camembert she'd brought from the market. Esme helped herself to a grape.

"Ahhh, you've caught us red handed, we're just settling in for the night," said Andrew, looking from his daughter to the table and rubbing his hands together. He picked up the wine bottle, peering at it over his spectacles which had dropped down his nose.

"I'm just about to open this splendid French Pinot Noir 2018 courtesy of Mr Flint."

Dougal was now sitting upright in his deckchair, nervously fiddling with his silk cravat.

"Oh it's just something I've had lying around. Didn't want it to go to waste," he muttered nonchalantly, his silvery mop neatly parted and combed to one side for the occasion. Esme was still perched on the floor, peering up at him from beneath her long lashes.

"I'm actually really glad I've caught you tonight Dougal," she said softly. She had the pendant he'd given her clutched tight between her fingers.

"I just wanted to say thank you so much for the baptisia necklace. It's beautiful. And it means so much that it once belonged to... well you know. I'll never take it off."

Buttercup had emerged from behind the herbs and was licking cheese from Dougal's hand. His hair had fallen back over his eyes which were fixed on the cat, but Esme could see he was smiling.

"You are very welcome my dear," he replied quietly but graciously.

"I thought that it was only right that it be returned to you and your family. You'll make far better use of it than me I'm sure."

There was a loud pop, as Andrew uncorked the wine, which made Esme laugh and Dougal clutch his chest and shout:

"Great sparks!"

"Steady on there Dougal," chortled Andrew, glugging large swathes of wine unsteadily into both of their glasses.

"As I said to Esme, I just can't believe you've kept it all these years. Such a fine day that was in the gardens all those years ago. The look on her face when she spotted the picnic under her favourite tree. And then when I finally got down on one knee and popped the question. Well... it was just magic. Anyway, cheers old boy," he said, plonking back down in his deckchair and raising his glass to his friend.

"And thank you to *you* for making that all possible."

Dougal peered out at him from beneath his hair, his mouth open in surprise. This was the most he had ever heard Andrew speak of Sienna since she had gone missing. And it was the first time she'd ever been mentioned on one of their Friday wine nights.

"Cheers," he replied, his voice full of wonder, clinking his glass against his friend's. He took a large mouthful of wine, which he swallowed with a loud gulp. Then he shuffled awkwardly in his deckchair, raising his eyes towards the stars, which were slowly lighting up one by one.

"Well you know…," he went on, his tone suddenly reflective.

"It was the least I could do for two people who were destined to be together. Like two trees 'whose roots are so entwined that it is inconceivable that you should ever part'.

Andrew slowly turned his head towards his friend, an eyebrow raised in admiration at his eloquent choice of words.

"Well said old boy," he replied.

"The wise words of Louis de Bernieres I believe?"

"They are indeed," Dougal mumbled distantly, still gazing at the night sky, before letting out an uneasy chuckle.

"Someone who also described love as a 'temporary madness'!"

Which made the others laugh nervously too, before falling back into subdued silence, the barge rocking them gently from side to side. How unimaginable and achingly sad it was that her parents' roots were no longer entwined, thought Esme, expecting the others were probably thinking the same. They sat quietly a minute longer, Andrew swirling his glass breathing in its heady notes and Dougal taking delicate sips, with his face still turned to the heavens. Esme was the first to break the silence.

"Speaking of…" she hesitated before going on.

"Mum."

The word caught the men off guard and made them look straight at her.

"I've been meaning to tell you something."

"Riiight?" said Andrew cautiously, placing his wine glass down so he could give her his full attention. Esme was shifting around on the floor, uncertain of where to start.

"Well," she went on.

"It's a curious thing really. It's just that I had the most peculiar dream. I was back in Avaley Hall, and Mum was there, although she wasn't a grown up, she was just a little girl. We were playing together in the nursery. It was a game of chess, although it wasn't really chess, it was a game she'd made up with a teddy bear called Aloysius and an invisible friend called Annabel."

"I see," said Andrew, his head now cocked to one side in amusement at his daughter's incessant rambling.

"But wait, there's more," Esme went on earnestly, holding her hand up.

"After we'd finished playing she suddenly ran into another room. Then when I followed her she was all grown up. Grandma was there and it was the morning of your wedding," she said, looking directly at her father.

"Okaaay," he replied slowly.

"And then what happened?"

"Well that's when I saw it," she said, as if it should by now be obvious.

"Saw what?" Andrew responded blankley.

"The first edition of Brideshead Revisited. In my dream. *That* was what you sent to her the morning of your wedding. She said that it was her favourite book."

Andrew's face had become ashen and his forehead wrinkled. His eyes had lost their sparkle and were swimming with confusion, while his jaw was opening and closing loosely as if wishing to speak. Not knowing what to say, he swallowed and started rubbing his stubble.

Esme's eyes then grew wide with shock.

"So it's true?" she asked her father in astonishment.

"Why didn't you tell me that was Mum's favourite book? Especially when I showed you the card? That was really important!"

Her voice was filled with hurt and resentment.

"I'm so sorry, petal…" Andrew pleaded sincerely.

"I thought that it was just a silly card. It really didn't seem that important. So many people quote Brideshead Revisited. Especially in Oxford. It was actually Dougal here who spotted the first edition of it for me in Last Bookshop in Jericho, all those years ago. You see it pops up everywhere! Perhaps I should have mentioned it. But I didn't want to upset you. Especially just after your birthday."

"But... but... how could you? And how could I have possibly known that?" Esme's eyes were now searching the table in confusion, as if she might find an answer somewhere there.

"Come along now Esmeralda," Dougal butted in, trying to diffuse the tension.

"You know that there's no truth in dreams. And you could save yourself a world of trouble by not bothering to look for any."

"But it *was* the truth," she snapped back.

"I can tell by Dad's face. It must have been some sort of prophecy or vision."

"Now now Esme, simmer down," said Andrew soothingly.

"You know full well there's no such thing. It was just a strange coincidence. We were just talking about the book earlier in the week weren't we? So no wonder it was still in your head."

Then leaning forward and grinning mischievously, he added:

"Unless you've been hanging out with that sorceress on that spooky barge. Watching her gaze into her crystal ball!"

He waved his hands and made a spooky "oooh" sound, trying to lighten the mood.

"Don't mock me Dad," said Esme, her voice stern.

"And anyway even if Hetty did have a crystal ball. Crystal balls predict the future. This was a dream about something that had already happened in the past which I didn't know about. How could that have happened? Unless crystal balls also work backwards?!"

At the mention of the word Hetty, Dougal had sat up straight in his chair. The others stared at him, waiting for him to elucidate.

"That woman," he said with a shudder.

"Can't say I know too much about her. But I'd keep as far away from her as possible if I was you. I don't like the look of her barge at all. Fancy calling it Asphodel of all things. Do you know what Asphodel is?"

Esme and Andrew both shook their heads vaguely.

"*Asphodelus ramosus,*" Dougal was now back on home turf, wrapping his mouth carefully around the Latin name.

"It's a grey flower, rather spiky and unappealing in my opinion. Connected to death and the underworld, according to Greek mythology. Or if you subscribe to the Victorian way of thinking, it literally means…"

He paused for dramatic effect, before continuing in a slow, monotonic voice:

"My regrets follow you to the grave."

Esme and Andrew looked at one another bleakly, although Andrew was secretly trying not to laugh at Dougal's overly affected gloominess. Then Andrew, suddenly remembering where he'd heard the name before, started steadily reciting:

"'Others in Elysian valleys dwell, Resting weary limbs at last on beds of asphodel.' Of course! Tennyson mentioned it too. Do you know I must have passed that barge a dozen times and never made the connection. I heard she was a showgirl in her younger days, and even had a brief engagement to a wealthy diamond dealer. She's led quite the exotic life by all accounts."

Then he noticed his daughter's heart shaped face, staring up at him, full of so much sadness it made his whole body hurt.

"Oh now come along Petal," he said gently, gazing into the bottomless green pools of her eyes.

"I am really sorry I didn't tell you about the book, it's just…"

"No really it's ok Dad," she interrupted calmly, shaking her head.

"I was actually just thinking about poor Hetty. Imagine living a life so full of regret that it consumes and tortures you like that. When her younger years were so glamorous and so much fun if you can believe the stories. I can't help thinking, what if she had never visited the Maison Souquet that night and met that Hollywood film director, how different her life may have turned out."

"Well we all have to live with our choices, Esmeralda," interrupted Dougal briskly.

"Which is why you should keep the baptisia pendant close and avoid those who may wish to lead you astray. Just one false move can bring the whole pack of cards tumbling down, you know."

At the mention of cards, Esme wondered whether she ought to mention the Tarot card Hetty had pinned to the barge. But thinking there had probably been enough drama for one night she decided to leave the men to enjoy their wine.

"Righty ho," she said breezily.

"Well I'm still no closer to finding out why I'm being sent these cards."

"Hang on a minute," Andrew said inquiringly.

"Did you just say cards? Do you mean to say there's been more than one?"

"Oh yes," answered Esme matter of factly.

"There was another one. And then a teddy bear. Mr Featherstone at Blackwells thought I'd left it there, because it had my name on it in that same green writing."

"A teddy bear too? How very odd!" her Dad exclaimed, scratching his head, looking thoroughly mystified.

"My goodness, one really doesn't know what to expect next in this sweet and strange city!"

"Yes, isn't that just the truth," Esme replied, pushing herself to her feet and rolling her eyes, more confused now than she had been earlier.

"Right and on that note, I'm off for an evening stroll to clear my head. Leave you gentlemen to enjoy your wine."

She was about to hop off the barge when she heard Dougal's tetchy voice calling after her:

"Oh Esmeralda. You are still coming to help me at the gardens tomorrow aren't you? The growth in the glass houses is as relentless as my hay fever in this tiresome warm weather."

"Yes, don't worry Dougal. I'll be there," she called back, flicking her hair over her shoulder and smiling back at him. Then she waved goodbye and jumped down to the towpath, watching the Flower Moon ripple in the water as she made her way down the river.

# Chapter 16 - Butterflies

Andrew and Dougal's voices slowly faded out as Esme walked away from Perditus Amor, and were replaced by a distant guitar. The moon was now high in the sky and she caught a sweet fragrance in the air as she drew closer to the music. Ahead of her was a powder blue barge she hadn't seen before, with the silhouette of a man in a cowboy hat sitting on its roof. It was bent over a guitar, plucking a Spanish sounding melody, surrounded by a hazy cloud of smoke. Then as Esme drew nearer, the music stopped.

"Hey," a drowsy voice called out from above. It was deep and husky with a slight crack in it. Esme glanced up, to see a man looking down, obscured by the front of his hat. He was inhaling on a long pipe coming from an ornate silver stand with a cut glass container of bubbling liquid at its base. He silently blew a musky plume of vapour into the air.

"Don't I know you from somewhere?" the voice carried on through the perfumed cloud. It was low and melodic yet strangely familiar.

"I don't think so," Esme mumbled back, lowering her head so that her hair fell in front of her face. She was about to hurry away, when the man pushed the hat up from his face with his forefinger.

"Yes I do know you," the voice went on, nodding through the smoke, making it break up and billow away.

"You're the girl with the teddy bear. Hey, and didn't you come to see my band?"

Esme was fixed to the spot as the vapour began to disperse, with memories of a song she wasn't familiar with until recently coming back to her in waves. And unless she was dreaming again, the voice it belonged to was speaking to her right now from a face with thick eyebrows, a chiselled jawline and shining blue eyes. *Those* shining blue eyes. Rafferty Montgomery knew who she was. Her mind was whirling, as she tried to fully comprehend why he was here and what was happening.

"Hey do you want some?" he asked, holding the pipe out towards her.

"Oh no thanks," she said shyly, about to walk away, when suddenly, the tune she'd heard at the ball started drifting from his fingers. She literally couldn't move. For the second time that week she was gazing up at Rafferty performing that song. Then he stopped and broke into a charming wide grin, leaning down and offering his hand.

"Jump up," he said. His tone was now playful and reassuring.

Esme glanced from left to right, to check no one was looking, then gingerly took his hand. She felt all his strength hoisting her up, and in one swift move was right up there next to him. He gestured to a red Moroccan cushion with golden tassels and she sat down.

"What's your name?" he asked softly, his eyes fixed on hers.

"Err Esme," she said. Her name suddenly sounded ridiculous to her own ear.

"Oh hang on aren't you Pr...?"

"Yep," she replied, nodding bashfully.

"Professor Drake's daughter."

"Cool," he said, running his fingers through his curls, before extending his hand.

"I'm Raff," he said.

"Hi Raff, it's nice to meet you," said Esme hesitantly, not sure whether to shake his hand or not, before cautiously taking it.

"Likewise," he said, flashing that amused grin she'd seen in Blackwells again.

"Hey, would you like something to drink? I've got whisky… or wine perhaps?" he went on, picking various bottles up from the roof of the barge then putting them down again.

"Errrr sure, wine sounds good," she said, not really sure that this was a good idea at all.

"White ok?"

She nodded, and he picked up a bottle then poured wine into two mismatched mugs.

"Cheers," he said, clinking his mug against hers and fixing her with his eyes.

"Cheers," she replied, trying to sound composed and grown up. Then they both took a slow mouthful of wine.

*What. Am. I. Doing?* thought Esme, feeling the liquid slide down her throat, easing her chest, before warming the pit of her stomach. Rafferty took another drag on his pipe then struck a match, held it in front of his eyes and peered into the flame. Then he lit a couple of silver lanterns to his left and his right and began to softly play the tune again. He was repeating a four bar bass line in a haunting minor key over and over while quietly humming the tune. Then, in a voice so broken she sensed the same sorrow she'd caught in his eyes, he sang a single line:

"And fade out again, fade out again."

Esme continued to listen as he went back to plucking out the acoustic bass line, his fingers long and agile across the strings.

"What is that?" she asked.

"It's so sad and yet so beautiful."

"You don't know it?" his mouth twisted into another amused smile.

"It's Radiohead. Street Spirit. I thought everyone knew this one."

Esme felt her cheeks sting. Of course she'd heard of Radiohead. He must think she was such a stupid child not to recognise the song.

"They're from Oxford you know," Raff went on, still playing.

"I always think there's something about their music, so dark and mysterious, that really captures the essence of this sublime place."

Esme nodded, still listening to him bringing out the evocative melody, her father's recent words about "this sweet and strange city," flowing back.

"It's like one day, you can be striding down the High, in the sweet summer sun, the sultry lines of a poem by Keats or Coleridge going round and round in your head. There's hope in your heart and you feel like you're floating on air. Then the next the sky turns cold and grey, the streets are gloomy and the old stone walls are getting higher and higher until the entire city is closing in on you. Nowhere to run and hide, constantly looking over your shoulder, everybody knows who you are and what your business is. And suddenly all you're left with is…"

Emptiness hovered in the air as Rafferty continued to play to the end of the bar then stopped. Esme noticed how young he looked at this moment, like a lost boy, in need of protection.

"Anyway," he went on, deliberately brightening his tone and placing his guitar down.

"That's more than enough of that. I want to know everything

about you."

His eyes were now fixed on her so intensely it made her mouth go dry and she was worried she might not be able to speak.

"Everything?" she asked sweetly, taking another sip of wine, which made him grin back at her with a suggestive arch of his eyebrow. He fixed his face and became serious again before continuing.

"So Esme Drake," he said her name slowly, giving his full attention to it.

"That's a lovely name. Although with a face like yours perhaps a more graceful bird, like a dove or a swan, might have suited you better as a surname. How fitting that you and your father should live down here on the river though. How do you find it?"

"Yeah it's ok," she said casually, trying not to show she was pleased with the compliment or sound too childlike.

"It's very peaceful, especially in the summer, you know. It's just us and the water and the creatures that live around us. Couldn't really imagine it any other way now."

"That's cool," he said mellowly, taking another long drag of his pipe.

"I absolutely love it down here," he went on, leaning back and pursing his lips to blow a thin line of smoke into the air. It curled upwards and Esme caught vanilla with a hint of spice, before it melted into the air.

"Oh and this old girl," he went on, giving the roof of the barge a gentle pat with his hand.

"Is Vita Somnium." He announced the name grandly.

"She belongs to my wonderfully unorthodox and endlessly endearing Aunt Phylis. She purchased it after her divorce from a ghastly little man from a small town in Sussex. It means 'Life is a Dream'," he added whimsically, before chuckling to himself at the irony. *How apt* thought Esme, her mind wandering through all the perplexing events of the past week, not least being sat here right now with this complex and mesmerising man.

"She's in the South of France this weekend visiting distant relatives, so she said I could come and hang out here. You know, get away from prying eyes and gossip," he added, raising his eyebrows seductively at the hint of bad behaviour. She wondered briefly what exactly he was running away from and where Rosaline might be this evening. She was trying her best not to allow her mind to wander and imagine that perhaps a break up was the cause of his low spirits.

"So that's me and her," he went on, although Esme now wasn't quite sure if he was referring to the boat, his aunt or Rosaline.

"So what do you do when you're not at the river? Hang on let me guess... I bet you're into books, nature, art... with an appreciation for everything that is fine and beautiful in the world. You must have been positively swathed in culture growing up with a father like yours. Hey...," he went on suddenly thinking of a common ground.

"Do you like poetry?"

Esme inwardly winced, thinking back to her disastrous recital at school, but decided to keep that memory to herself. So she simply nodded and said:

"I do. I love it."

Then he pulled his legs under him so he was sitting cross legged and closed his eyes. He took a deep breath then started to recite in his deep, husky voice:

"Never give all the heart,

For love will hardly seem worth thinking of,

To passionate women, if it seem

Certain, and they never dream

That it fades out from kiss to kiss."

Esme laughed quietly at this, but never took her eyes from his lips as he was speaking.

"Yes I know that one," she said softly.

"W. B. Yeats. Giving the old treat 'em mean to keep 'em keen advice. 'For everything that's lovely is but a brief, dreamy, kind delight,' and all that," she went on sarcastically, rolling her eyes.

"And I suppose that's your philosophy, is it Raff? Always hold something back. Keep them on their toes?"

Feeling emboldened by the wine she raised a flirtatious eyebrow back at him.

"Touchee!" he crooned, sounding slightly pompous and revealing his aristocratic roots for the first time that evening. Then, throwing his head back and letting out a deep belly laugh he went on:

"Heavens no, I wish I didn't always have to give all of my heart. But sadly I am and always will be a hopeless romantic."

He flicked his hair away from his face and held her with his eyes again.

"That said, there might be hope for me yet. I guess we're all constantly learning and evolving aren't we? Toughening up our outer shells, going through our messy years, like a chrysalis, before spreading our wings like… well you know."

He left another blank space hanging between them. Esme, now light headed from the wine, pictured Rafferty morphing into a rainbow of moving colours, like a kaleidoscope, before unfolding two beautiful large wings. She swallowed a mouthful of wine, gazed directly into his eyes, then recited four short lines slowly back to him:

"I've watched you now a full half-hour,

Self-poised upon that yellow flower

And - little Butterfly! Indeed

I know not if you sleep or feed."

Rafferty looked at her for some time, rendered speechless by her innocence. Esme was blushing, hoping the words hadn't sounded too juvenile, while twirling a strand of her hair around and around her finger. She had watched him, sitting in the moonlight, playing music and speaking like one of the romantic poets for a good half hour. Yet to her he was still simply the most wonderful enigma.

"Wordsworth," he said finally, looking at her like a lost boy once again. Then, just as she was opening her mouth to say yes, he put his hand through her auburn locks and kissed her. In a flash, Esme was back in Christchurch Meadow, lying in the grass, watching the sky light up with a thousand fireworks and stars. Then, after a moment or two, her mind suddenly became calm, quiet and clear. Just like the lotus flower, emerging out of the chaos and opening its pure white petals to the sun.

He pulled away and looked directly into her eyes again. There was still electricity shooting down her arms to her fingertips but her mind was peaceful bliss. Then, glancing down at the watch her dad had given for her birthday, she suddenly noticed the time.

"Oh gosh," she said.

"I hadn't realised it was getting so late.

"Hey," he said, gently rubbing her arm.

"No worries. D'you need me to walk you home?"

"No," she said softly.

"We're literally just over there," she added, pointing to lights and smoke coming from the roof of her barge where her Dad and Dougal were still sitting out smoking cigars.

"When can I see you again?" he went on urgently.

"Hey, I'll be swinging by college tomorrow to grab some books. You could come and pick me up from the library, say around 3? Then we could grab coffee or something. Maybe walk back to the river together?"

That word. *"Together"*. Was Rafferty Montgomery actually asking her out on a date? Now Esme knew she really must be dreaming.

"Ahhh sure," she whispered back, hoping that she hadn't misheard him.

"Cool," he said, giving her another peck on the lips.

"Well tonight was lovely," she said, desperately wishing she could stay a little longer.

"But I really must be getting home."

"Sure thing," he said softly, his hand still cupping her face.

"Tomorrow at 3 though?"

"Tomorrow at 3." She nodded, looking up at him timidly from beneath her eyelashes. Then he ran his hands through his hair, put two fingers to his lips and blew her a kiss, as she swung her legs off the side of the barge and jumped onto the toe path. Then she drifted back down the river like she was floating on clouds with the strumming of a guitar fading back into the distance.

# Chapter 17 – The Water Lily House

"Morning moon," Esme mumbled sleepily to the large orb painted above her head. Awakening to her celestial ceiling, she felt quite certain her evening of music and romance had been another dream. She'd returned to the barge to find her father and Dougal tipsy and animated, quarrelling over the merits of the British legal system, so had quietly taken herself to bed. But when she closed her eyes, images of those sultry sapphires stopped her from falling asleep. And if slumber prevailed, mesmeric butterflies would flutter towards her, then evaporate into pastel puffs of smoke. She'd woken up drowsy from trying to catch them before they disappeared.

But now she was watching the river's ripples reflected on her ceiling, thinking what a wonderful dream it had been. She stretched and yawned and caught a smoky taste of vanilla and wine in her mouth. And that's when she knew for sure. She *had* sat on the rooftop reciting poetry with Rafferty. And not only that... they'd kissed!

Rolling over and spotting the time, she quickly leapt out of bed. She'd promised Dougal that she would help him at the gardens and then Rafferty had asked to meet her. Rafferty Montgomery actually wanted to see her again. She giggled to herself then shook her hair over her face, willing herself not to get too carried away. Pulling on a cotton dressing gown and grabbing Aloysius from the end of the bed, she plodded drowsily to the centre of the barge. Plonking him on the kitchen table, she grabbed a post-it note and scribbled:

"The mystery bear... both sweet and strange!"

Then she stuck it on the teddy's head for her Dad to see when he woke up, and traipsed cheerfully back to her bedroom.

It was 11am by the time Esme left the barge. She'd chopped and changed her mind several times over a suitable choice of outfit. It needed to be *practical* for The Gardens, and *flattering but not too showy*
for meeting Rafferty at the library. After trying numerous jumpers and blouses, with the only three pairs of trousers she owned, she'd eventually settled for a lavender skirt which flowed to her ankles with a simple white t-shirt. She pulled the Baptisia necklace out so it was proudly on show, smoothed her hair back with Freddy's scarf, and made her way down the river.

It was another gloriously warm May day, with swallows swooping low over Christ Church Meadow, heralding the news that Summer had arrived. Hawthorn bushes were awash with white blossom with intrepid wild roses creeping up between. And the final flourishes of Spring's cherry blossom, floated down like confetti, before drifting away down the Cherwell to the Thames. Still hazy from broken sleep, Esme wandered along as if she were walking in a dream. And each time a butterfly fluttered her way she felt sure she was still in a world of fantasy. But seeing the sturdy stone archway into The Gardens brought her back to the reality of the day.

Making her way towards the tranquil fountain delicately cascading into a round pond, she spotted a small figure shuffling up the path behind it. It was tugging a moth eaten shawl around a faded dress, which was frayed and torn above its clumpy boots. Coarse hair was heaped on its head in a matted bun while a worn willow basket filled with heather and herbs swung from its wrist. As it drew closer it let out a satisfied cackle, which instantly unveiled its identity.

"So we meet again, my beauty!"

Hetty had spiralled around the fountain before Esme had a chance to escape. She appeared in her path like a bat out of hell, with the water flowing behind her like wings.

"And looking ravishing as always," she went on, brushing loose tendrils of hair from her pallid face, while casting jealous eyes hastily up and down Esme's body.

"What's the occasion my dear? Don't tell me you've dressed up for *him*? I trust you received my small floral gift and my word of warning?" she added keenly, scuffling uncomfortably close to Esme while awaiting an agreeable response.

"Your stupid tarot card?" Esme replied angrily, stepping away and folding her arms protectively over her body.

"Beware the Dark Stranger?"

She repeated the words slowly and sarcastically, making them sound absurd.

"You think you can scare me with words like those do you? Who do you think you are? And what made you think you could come near my barge?"

Hetty bent her small frame over, pulling the basket's handle beneath her chin with her eyes innocently wide.

"Not to scare you my dear. It was a warning. Goddesses must protect one another," she said, in a voice that was sickly sweet but which made her more sinister to Esme than before.

"But seeing you here dressed like *that*, it would appear that my words fell on deaf ears. Or that you are trying to provoke me. Or even worse… entice him?" she went on, lunging back into Esme's personal space, her condemning eyes burning like coals. Esme started to laugh wearily, though she could feel her cheeks flushing.

"Entice who? Rafferty?" she said incredulously.

"I'm doing nothing of the sort. He's just a friend."

"*Raffety…?*"

Hetty repeated the name with wonder, like it was the first time she had ever heard it, before throwing her head back with a venomous cackle.

"So that's what he's calling himself these days is it? First it was Balthazar, then Jeremiah. I suppose Rafferty is some veiled attempt to cover his tracks…"

"Tracks?" Esme said tersely, tired and frustrated of Hetty's taunts.

"What tracks? What on earth are you talking about Hetty?"

Hetty drew herself up in front of Esme so they were almost eye to eye.

"Talking… Talking??" she said snarkily, cocking her head to one side with contempt.

"Talk is cheap!" she barked as angrily as a hellcat.

"Seeing is believing my dear. Come to me at Asphodel this

evening and I shall reveal everything you need to know. And then this Rafferty and his games will be out of your life... forever!"

She screeched the last word, clutching her shawl to her chest with a bony fist, and swung past Esme so fast she almost knocked her over. Then she shuffled off towards the stone arch, muttering gratifyingly to herself all the way, before pausing to rasp "I'll be waiting dear," then disappearing into the street.

Esme had heard stories about Hetty travelling the country, giving clumps of heather out to strangers for luck, but she had never seen her collecting it from the Gardens before. It suddenly seemed like she was following her everywhere. She thought about what Summer had said in the dining room about hiring an investigator to find out who her "Stalker" was. There would be no need, she thought, as she had pretty much revealed herself!

"So much for covering tracks," she mumbled crossly to herself as she made her way along a gravel path to the glass houses.

Despite haunting her like a phantom these days, Esme still couldn't be certain whether Hetty was behind the mystery cards and teddy bear. But the thought of going to Asphodel to find out more filled her with dread, especially when she'd been so frightening and forceful there before. And would she find out something terrible about Rafferty if she did?

"No," she said to herself, spotting the old greenhouses clustered together by the river, their angular surfaces glistening like gemstones, making her feel emboldened.

"This is just another one of Hetty's silly tricks. You have plans with Rafferty tonight and she's just jealous. You can't let a crazy old harradon's bitterness spoil that."

Just saying the words "plans with Rafferty," made her heart flutter and she broke into a meek smile. But it was at times like this that she desperately longed to have her Mother back. She'd never actually had a boyfriend, as Freddy loved to constantly remind her. And even she knew that the last woman she should be taking advice on men from was Hetty!

Wandering past the fronts of the glass houses she saw a familiar grey mop, tending to a pond of graceful green pads floating on an indoor pond. Dougal once told her that, as a Pisces, he was at his most "blithesome and unperturbed" in The Water Lily House, which is also why he could unwind so easily on Perditus Amor. Esme suspected the serenity of the latter may have more to do with a liquid which poured from a bottle rather than one which floated down the river. However, quietly walking in and letting the tropical heat of The Water Lily House envelop her, she felt her soul settle too. She was safe again.

"There you are dear," Dougal said, with uncommon pleasantry, turning around and glancing down at his watch.

"I was starting to worry. It's not like you to be late."

Esme shook her head and lifted the pendant around her neck with a contented smile.

"Well there's no need to worry, is there now Dougal?" she said assuredly.

"Not when a dear friend has given me such a wonderful talisman."

Dougal immediately blushed and hid behind his hair, flapping his hand at her to: "Give over!"

"Actually Dougal... I believe it may have already worked its powers today. It was actually that woman we were talking about on Friday who held me up," Esme went on.

"Woman?" Dougal interjected, pulling his hair back with both hands like he was parting curtains and blinking his magnified eyes.

"Yes Hetty," Esme went on calmly.

"She was here. Leaving with a huge basket full of herbs and all sorts of things."

"Here?" Dougal asked incredulously, his eyes now as wide as the lily pads.

"Here at the gardens? With herbs and things you say? That witch? That maleficent woman from Asphodel?" he added, getting increasingly flustered. He took an inhaler from his pocket and drew on it with a loud wheeze.

"Yes," said Esme, wondering for the first time if the "dark stranger" she'd referred to was actually Hetty herself. She wouldn't put it past her to play a joke on her like that. In fact after this morning, she wouldn't put anything past her really.

"But don't worry," she said, as if soothing a frightened child. She knew that if there was one thing Dougal liked less than new people, it was new people who petrified him appearing on his territory. It had taken him a fortnight to recover after Mr Bartholmew brought a group of biochemistry students to study the Venus Fly Traps in The Carnivorous Plants House.

"She's gone now," Esme went on kindly, gently rubbing Dougal's arm.

"I think she was just stopping off to pick up some heather you know. She moves around the country handing it out for luck apparently. She'll be off and away in a few days stocking up elsewhere. Goodness knows where in the world she'll end up."

"Luck…?" Dougal said, his augmented eyes now narrowing with suspicion.

"That's rich. I wouldn't be surprised if she hasn't cast one of her charms on it. In order to bewitch some poor soul, and most likely ruin their life!"

"Come on now Dougal, that's a bit harsh," said Esme reprovingly, although she knew it wasn't unlike Dougal to get carried away when he was having a grumble about someone.

"I thought you said you didn't know much about her?"

"Well I don't, dear," Dougal added hastily.

"It's just you know how I feel about…"

He lowered his voice and glanced around to check no one was listening.

"Magic… Especially of the blackened variety. Knowing plants and herbs the way that I do, I mean. With all their special… you know…properties," he added, sounding as cloak and dagger as if he were telling her where he'd hidden the key to the Crown Jewels.

"All that I'm saying is that I am fully aware that there are those who choose to use them for…"

He paused for dramatic effect:

"Malevolent and nefarious wrongdoing," he declared solemnly and superiorly, lowering his head, before blinking rapidly behind his chunky glasses to gauge Esme's reaction. Brightening his tone a little, he added:

"So just keep the baptisia close my dear. And stay away from that woman!"

Esme usually found Dougal's lectures, with their deadpan seriousness and ostentatious language, quite amusing. But the fact that he had been thoughtful enough to give her her mother's necklace, and was so concerned for her safety melted her heart.

"Always Dougal," she replied softly, wrapping her fingers around the pendant and giving him a wink.

Dougal quietly wandered off, leaving Esme staring at her reflection amongst the water lilies faced up like giant tea trays. Maybe it was just the way the sunlight was shimmering across the water, but she thought she looked a little different today.

She paused to think about all the other recent changes and the new people who had come into her life. Hetty, Rafferty, Rupert… even her Mum seemed somewhat new now she knew a little more about her. They'd also helped her discover new parts of herself: resilience to fight off Hetty, stamina to keep up with Rupert and a mix of feelings she didn't even know how to describe for Rafferty. Despite all this, she still hadn't quite worked out who she was, let alone who was behind the mystery cards.

Still gazing into the pond, she saw delicate pink-white flowers rising between the water lilies, unfolding their petals to bright rays of sun streaming through the glass. And that's when it all became clear:

"I'm a lotus flower…" she whispered, with a sense of calm enlightenment and a knowing smile.

## Chapter 18 - Dust

Esme had hoped her sense of calm and serenity would last until it was time to meet Rafferty. But as is so often the way with best laid plans, it didn't. Once she'd hacked sugarcane in The Rainforest House, repotted geraniums in The Conservatory, and listened to Dougal spout more than the fountain about ferns browning in The Cloud Forest, she felt weary and a little unkempt. Plus her wavy hair had done what it generally did when faced with humidity: frizz! But seeing the delicate hands of her antique watch approaching three o'clock, she removed her apron and made her way towards Teddy Hall.

Turning by the coffee house on Queen's Lane and seeing her window table lying empty, she longed to just grab a latte and hole up with a novel for the next few hours. But since she'd made a promise she knew she'd regret breaking, she continued resolutely on to the college.

Teddy Hall's library was housed in a 12th century mediaeval church nestled behind the front quad. It had a soaring square tower, visible from Queen's Lane, and ancient rubble walls. Esme crept through a stone archway next to the bar, onto a path winding through a primitive graveyard. She used to find its crooked tombstones, sunk down to moss covered stubs after centuries of standing, a little eerie and macabre. But these days she found it a tranquil space, and loved to lie in the shade of its yew trees and daydream. But approaching the church's Galilee porch with its looming oak doors today, Esme felt as apprehensive as if she'd agreed to sleep in the crypt. Plus it was such a hurried plan, she now wasn't sure if Rafferty had said he'd meet her inside or out. Since she didn't actually have a key to the library there was little other option than to wait.

Esme stood and watched earnest students come and go and huddle in groups on blankets around the burial ground. She saw a jackdaw swoop onto a crumbling tomb, wings spread like a black cloak, before tucking them behind its back and eyeing her suspiciously like Mr Bartholomew. Then caught a plucky robin making battle with a strong willed worm in the shadow of a headstone. By the time the bird had valiantly conquered, the city bells announced it was half past the hour, and Esme felt almost as tormented as his victim. What if Rafferty didn't know she hadn't got a key and thought she'd just stood him up? He'd probably assume she could borrow her father's and might be waiting inside just like her. Seeing no other choice, she waited for a timid girl in corduroy culottes and one of Hyacinth's blouses, to open the door and covertly followed her in.

Esme had walked beneath the stone pillars and Norman arches of the library many times, but never alone nor with her pulse racing faster than Rupert on a bicycle. Nervously walking down a red carpet where the aisle once lay, she felt as reticent as a runaway bride. She scanned reading desks on either side where the devout and the pious once sat in elementary pews and prayed beneath towering church windows. But there was no sign of Rafferty. With her heart in her boots, she turned to leave and collided with a figure bearing a mountain of books.

"I'm so sorry!" she blurted, crouching down, frantically trying to collect them, before spotting a head of thick curly black hair which was doing the same. Sensing it was being watched, it looked up and fixed her with the same eyes that had shone by the light of the moon before infiltrating her dreams.

"Hey," he said, just as he had when gazing down at her from the roof of his aunt's barge in his cowboy hat. With all the butterflies of the night before flooding back, Esme was about to reply, when the sound of an upper class woman's voice behind him cut her off:

"Raffy! Hurry up darling. I need those books asap or else I'll be late for my Pilates class."

With all of her worst fears rising in her chest Esme looked up, to find a beautiful woman glaring down at them, with long blonde hair, so perfect, it made her feel like a savage.

"Yeah sorry Ros. I just ran into…"

Rafferty was about to submit an innocent plea when Rosaline Carmichael shot him down with her judgement:

"Professor Drake's kid. Yes I can see that. How sweet of you to come and collect books for your Daddy."

Esme felt a punch to her guts so powerful it left her utterly floored, with a physical pain inflamed by anger and humiliation. She burned with the impulse to flee from the library, but her pride and indignation kept her rooted. Rafferty had invited her here and she certainly wasn't going to let him see her crumble. Not wishing to embarrass herself further she calmly pulled herself up, looked Rosaline in the eye, and said:

"Excuse me please. I need to get through," before silently passing her, head held high, then disappearing into the nearest row of bookcases.

As soon as Esme was safely concealed within a private cavern of printed work, she felt the heat of her tears threatening to erupt. How could she possibly have been so stupid? Everyone from Priya to Freddy and even Hetty had warned her not to trust

Rafferty. It was common knowledge that he and Rosaline were in love and always ended up getting back together. And as if she could compete with a woman so elegant with her gardeners nails and dishevelled hair. Just as her tears were on the brink of falling and offering her solace, her rival's cut glass whisper made its way into her sanctum.

"I didn't know that you knew her," Rosaline said derisively, in a voice that was hushed but meant to be heard.

"You've heard about her family haven't you? It's *such* a scandal. First her father starts spending too much time with his students and staying up until all hours. Then her mother mysteriously vanishes. And now him and the girl are flat out broke and living on some ramshackle boat somewhere. Toby Newgent reckons he's seen the professor throwing roses into the river on May morning. I mean you don't do that unless you know something do you? So I reckon she must be dead. It's always the husband. Isn't that what they say?"

Rosaline hammered her final nail into the coffin with a blow so callous it left Esme tearing towards the door and gasping for air.

"Esme wait!" Rafferty called out behind her, feeling the pain of the sweet girl he'd recited poetry with as keenly as if he'd just stabbed a dove. But it was too late. Esme swung the time worn doors open with such ferocity they crashed into the walls with a sound which could have raised the dead. Then she ran through the cemetery, as her dreams turned to dust, leaving her betrayer and her baiter behind her.

# Chapter 19 - With love, Henrietta

*"Beware the Dark Stranger".*

Hetty's stark warning, so clear and so explicit, went round in Esme's head as she fled from Teddy Hall. She'd been so wrapped up in her infatuation with Rafferty she'd failed to see signs literally spelled out in front of her. Once again, she'd been trying so hard to see the branches that she'd missed the detail and clarity of the leaves. As she wound alongside the Cherwell River, with her heart tender and her spirit bruised, their green had never looked so vibrant nor so lucent.

"Why didn't I see this coming?" she mumbled, with moments that led to that torturous scene playing over and over in her mind. Christ Church Meadow, now rolling beside her, took her right back to the May Ball and the first flutter of a butterfly's wings. Then the mystery envelopes which sent her to Blackwell's, beguiling and coaxing her towards a shadow in a doorway. And then a dream, a forgotten grasshopper and an unknown aunt's divorce, edging two lost and lonely strangers together on a moonlit evening. Each moment a tiny cloud never to form again, yet all now infinitely set in the stratosphere of time. As the Cherwell's waters made their way into the Thames, Esme wondered where it was that she might be flowing. Making her way down the riverbank towards Perditus Amor she spotted a plume of black smoke, twisting up like a sea dragon, and felt tempted to enter its lair.

*"Come to me at Asphodel… and I shall reveal everything,"* Hetty had

said at the gardens. *Not that there could be much more to find out,* Esme thought. After Rafferty's deception and Rosaline's cruelty, she could understand why Hetty had tried to protect her. But what had she meant by Rafferty calling himself Balthazar and Jeremiah? And in what way had he been *"covering his tracks"*?

Esme thought about her father teasing her about Hetty's crystal ball and felt an unfamiliar jolt of anger and resentment. She rarely felt anything other than love for her Dad. But Rosaline's horrifying assumption had left her enraged and distressed.

*Is that really what people think about us around here?* Esme thought, getting chills imagining the eyes of the college prying into their hideaway on the barge. Hetty had already warned her against one man but what if her crystal ball needed to illuminate another? With a head as full of confusion as it was trepidation, Esme decided it was finally time to give in to the lady of Asphodel and enter her mysterious world.

"Hetty..." she called, as she cautiously crept onto the bow of her barge which lurched with a menacing creak. The front was as tumbledown with weeds as the roof, with a sorrowful angel statue weeping beneath her wings at the peak. One look at it and Esme immediately felt like she was back in the cemetery. She spotted small shabby doors behind trailing ivy and a tasselled dream catcher and hesitantly knocked three times. There was no answer. She was tempted to walk away. But seeing smoke still billowing from a rusty chimney, knowing she would never be fired up or brave enough to confront Hetty again, she felt around for two brass knobs and steadily opened the doors.

"Oh my goodness," she whispered as her eyes slowly focussed on the shadowy wonderland within. Unlike Perditus Amor with its fresh cream walls and cheerful furnishings, Asphodel was as dark as its name. But while the perishing plants and fallen angel outside had seemed maudlin, the interior held a certain lustre. The walls were painted the richest of scarlets covered in old posters dusky from smoke. Can-can dancers kicked their legs beneath layers of frilly skirts, while knickerbockered acrobats somersaulted over lions and clowns.

*"Come To The Enchanted Big Top!"* was blazoned above many, with *"Buy tickets now..."* scribbled below.

Esme caught the smell of aromatic spice drifting from an old copper pot bubbling on a cast iron stove. Ramshackle wooden shelves above it were stuffed with jars of dried seeds and herbs, with bunches of lavender, heather and thistles hanging from hooks below.

"Damiana, Fumitory, Belladonna," Esme whispered, as she slowly ran her finger along the handwritten labels. Remembering the more commonly known name of the latter she blurted:

"Deadly nightshade!" then shuddered at its potential danger.

Stepping away from Hetty's toxic kitchen, Esme wandered towards a dressing area at the end of the barge. Having only ever seen Hetty in threadbare shawls and tatty dresses she marvelled at the charm of her boudoir. An ebony vanity table with a velvet surface and ornate candlesticks was covered in her decorative belongings: hand-painted silk scarves with fine tassels draped over an oval mirror; perfume bottles encrusted with jewels clustered in a corner; and a crystal powder jar with a large swans-down puff clutched by a tiny silver claw. There was a cushion shaped like a pumpkin filled with hat pins adorned with peacock feathers; a silver skull; a ruby heart; a china teapot; a diamond crucifix; a glass eye; an emerald shamrock; an onyx cat and an opal. And Hetty's tarot cards were neatly piled to one side by a copper vase of wilting roses. But there was no sign of a crystal ball.

The walls were covered in postcards from everywhere from Paris to New York and Rome as well as black and white Polaroid pictures. Esme leaned in, carefully studying each of them by the dim light of the stove. There was a woman laughing and waving on an elephant then running riotously across a beach with a friend. In another she shaded her eyes reclining on a yacht, then sat beneath a sycamore smoking a cigarette with a guitar. Esme found her again on a poster, wearing a black tutu on pointed toes with hair slicked back in a bun. Her arms were softly arched overhead and her chin was modestly lowered. But her winged eyes looked up, burning into the camera, mesmerising with their beauty. Elegant handwriting swirling below said:
With love, Henrietta X."

Just as Esme was starting to lose herself in the glamour and romance of Hetty's former life, she heard the doors fly open and a rasping voice shout:

"What are you doing in my Kingdom?!"

Esme spun around in a panic.

"I'm so sorry Hetty, I just…" she stuttered.

But it was too late, Hetty was storming towards her with a face like thunder.

"I clearly instructed you to meet me at Asphodel *this evening*!" she screeched.

"It's still daylight. You're far too early. And you have no business being in Asphodel alone."

"I'm so sorry…" Esme attempted again. But Hetty was already leering up in her face, so she was jammed against the dressing table, trying hard not to sit on a hat pin.

"And what if 'The Stranger' had seen you?" she chided.

"Followed you I mean? This is strictly women's business. And I certainly don't need *him* darkening my door!"

"You mean Rafferty?" Esme asked timidly.

"Look Hetty, I already know all about him…"

"Rafferty, Ignasius, Phoenix, Atticus…"

Hetty was reeling names off like a twisted nursery rhyme.

"I've heard it all before! He'll try anything to cast off the title that belies his true nature."

Esme shook her head in confusion, but Hetty was now pacing back up the barge, making it rock unsteadily and the pot on the stove spill its contents.

"Now look here," she shouted, lifting the lid so steam hit her face and liquid bubbled over with a scorching hiss.

"I've brewed a special potion for you. For protection. Now it's nothing too elaborate. Just a little Blessed Thistle mixed with Horsetail and Irish Moss, a spot of Skullcap, a dash of Mandrake and a measure of Marshmallow Root."

Esme nodded, while attempting to look appreciative of the boiling slime being presented like a gourmet meal. Hetty slammed the lid back down then scurried back, linking Esme's arm and tugging her towards the door.

"Now you listen to me. Return to me at Asphodel after dusk

dear," she muttered urgently.

"Where you shall drink my potion beneath the moon and stars. Then I can reveal the source of your torment, once we're certain that the coast is clear."

Then she shoved Esme out of the barge, making her trip on the way, and slammed the doors behind her with a bang. Esme stood on the bow with her heart racing and her mind spinning as it tried to keep up. She'd always known Hetty could be volatile and that visiting her at Asphodel was a risk. But she'd been so blindsided by the incident in the library that her desperation for answers had driven her there anyway. But now, if it were humanly possible, she felt even more wretched than before. She looked down at the woeful weeping angel sitting amongst the broken pots and dying geraniums looking as alone and dejected as she felt. Without warning tears started pouring down her cheeks, dropping off her chin like the heavy rain drops that follow a scorching heat wave. And then her legs were running towards her last remaining safe haven: the tiny port in a storm that was Perditus Amor.

## Chapter 20 - Venice

"At least I've still got you Puss," Esme said despondently, looking at Buttercup curled up on her lap as she sat with her legs dangling over the side of the barge. After racing back to Perditus Amor she'd gone straight to the roof, eager for spaciousness after the shady confines of Asphodel and its cantankerous owner. The familiar sight of the trees standing firm on the riverbank and boats passing by with people getting on with life, blissfully unaware that hers was in tatters, had gone some way to making her feel more grounded. But after being hurt by Rafferty, Rosaline and Hetty all in one day, she really wasn't sure who to trust anymore. It brought that excruciating moment in the library flooding back, and the torrent of her tears to the fore.

"Perhaps I just need to be a bit more cat," she mumbled through her sniffles.

"Just like you Buttercup. Wild and independent. Unfettered by the opinions of others. Not to mention preening myself more..." she added gloomily, glancing at the ends of her hair. Remembering Rosaline's perfect tresses, she felt the heat of her tears rise again.

"Yes," she continued firmly, before they could fall.

"From now on I intend to be detached and unflappable. As well as attempting to get more sleep," she added, with an emphatic nod to her cat who was happily snoozing.

"You're actually quite the maverick now I come to think of it Buttercup. So when in doubt I will just channel you. And remain completely unemotional at all times."

Then her sobs erupted again, with tears so big she could see them landing in the river. Esme couldn't remember the last time she'd cried like this. Probably not since she was very small. It seemed that ever since she'd become a year older, she somehow felt more childlike than before.

"Why does it all have to be so hard?" she moaned, as Buttercup rolled onto her back and leisurely stretched out one of her paws. It reminded her of what Priya had said about her trying too hard to remember the words to the poem. With that in mind, and having had quite the day, she decided to go to her room for a lie down.

Sitting on her bed, with her crocheted blanket wrapped around her, she gazed out of her porthole, hoping the sight of a Great Crested Grebe swimming or a Cormorant swooping might perk her up. But there was nothing there. And now she came to think of it, something didn't seem quite right. It looked like the water was getting higher, moving up towards the top of the window. Just as she was about to take a closer look, she heard a crack, and then a thunderous shatter as her porthole smashed to smithereens, allowing the river to cascade in. She tried to leap off her bed, but it was too late. The water was filling her room, pulling her in with its current, dragging her towards the painting at the end of her bed.

Everywhere went murky and cold and she could feel her body swirling in chaos, just like being sucked down a giant plug hole. She was finding it hard to breathe and was starting to panic, terrified she might drown. Suddenly her stomach flipped over, just like it had when she fell down the well, and she could feel herself falling, falling, falling. Until everything flashed bright white and she hit the ground.

Curled up in a foetal position Esme felt weak and disoriented, with her head spinning and her ears ringing. She could still hear the sound of water, but it seemed like the torrent of the flood had been replaced by something gentler, like a soft lapping noise. The warmth of the sun was beating down on her back with a soft texture beneath her face. As she slowly, slowly opened her eyes she discovered that she had landed on a white velvet cushion. Then easing herself up she realised, to her complete astonishment, that she was sitting in an ornate gold gondola.

The light was intensely bright all around, with water below, and walls soaring either side. With her eyes slowly adjusting to the glare she realised there was no gondolier, just a woman sitting opposite in long white robes. Instantly recognizing the face, so similar to her own, Esme gasped, then whispered:

"Mum?"

Sienna Drake looked more radiant than ever. Her auburn hair rolled in soft waves down to her waist and her eyes were beaming with love:

"Hello my dear," she said, with her voice calm and her face relaxed.

"I can't tell you how wonderful it is to see you again after all these years."

Esme noticed they were drifting towards a bridge, with bright white light pouring through it.

"Are we in? Are we in h, h…? she stuttered nervously.

"Heaven? Well I guess you could say that darling. We're in my idea of heaven," she said laughing delightfully. To Esme it sounded like a thousand cherubs and instantly made her feel calm and safe.

"No this is Venice silly," her mother went on.

"It's where your father and I honeymooned. Plus, I'll let you in on a little secret. We kissed right under this bridge," she whispered conspiratorially, pointing up to the bridge which was right above their heads.

"The Bridge of Sighs. Your father was never one for superstition but I believed in the old tradition that those who kiss beneath it will share an eternal love."

As they emerged from the other side of the bridge, Esme immediately looked around her. The walls had now disappeared and there was no water beneath them. They were still steadily moving, but everything around the gondola was just bright white light. But Sienna didn't seem to notice. She just kept gazing at Esme with her beautiful green eyes.

"We spent the weekend here before heading to Lake Garda, such a heavenly place," she went on.

"Your father would get up early for a swim in the lake then be back to wake me up at eight with a breakfast of boiled eggs, toast soldiers, coffee and freshly squeezed orange juice. He'd bring them in on a tray with a single white rose and the morning paper folded neatly beside it. We'd take them out onto our balcony and watch the sun slowly rising above the lake. Then we'd pack a bag with books, wine, bread and cheese and stretch out by the pool for the rest of the day, surrounded by mountains and peaceful waters. Those were some of the laziest and happiest days of my life. I didn't think that it was earthly possible for my heart to feel any fuller.

Until that is you came along. We found out I was pregnant on your father's birthday. You were the perfect present, our precious little wildflower, due on May Day. But you always kept us on our toes and arrived a day earlier than expected. I remember how you came into the world like a force of nature, your little arms and legs flailing like a lioness protecting her young. Holding you in my arms for the very first time, swaddled in a blanket with your big eyes and button nose poking out, it was like discovering the garden of Eden.

Then we took you home to our house in Summertown. Our little Utopia as we used to call it. I'd covered the walls with rolls of floral paper I'd found in the attic and your father had fixed up some antique furniture he'd got for a steal at a salvage yard in Abingdon. He'd regularly be up until the early hours and wouldn't rest until that beautiful grandfather clock in the hallway was ticking again. And my father even had my old rocking horse and piano from Avaley Hall delivered to us as a surprise after our honeymoon. It was always a home filled with music, laughter and love.

Then your Dad converted the shed at the end of the garden into my study so that I could work on my novels, and keep an eye on you when you were playing in the garden with Buttercup. You'd often burst in laden with gifts of jam sandwiches, insects in jars and bunches of flowers, and do you know what you used to say to me? You used to grab my face in both your little hands and say:

"I love you Mummy. You were my very first friend."

And I would gaze at you, my little ray of sunshine, and think to myself:

"If it could only be like this always – always summer,"

Then Sienna closed her eyes and turned her face towards the bright light, with her mouth set in a blissful smile, like she was basking in the sunshine.

Seeing her mother like that, Esme suddenly felt an uneasy sensation in the pit of her stomach. The way Sienna was gently swaying with the gondola, her eyes closed in reverie, seemed like she'd slipped into a trance and was drifting away. Wanting to hold her mother in this moment forever Esme cried out, desperate to wake her and bring her back:

"But where have you been all these years Mum?"

But it was too late. The light was getting brighter and brighter and Sienna was slowly fading away. Until she was finally gone. And then in a flash the gondola was gone too and Esme was falling, falling, falling once again.

But this time she didn't feel afraid and she wasn't falling into darkness. The bright light was still all around and she was drifting down, as gently as a swan's feather. She closed her eyes then felt herself land on a soft surface, wrapped in a warm blanket of peace.

She'd met her mother. But not as a child this time, as the woman who had carried, given birth to her and loved her. It warmed her soul to hear Sienna's melodic voice, telling her what life had been like when she was a little girl, like she was reading her a bedtime story. Her father never talked much about the old days. She wished so much that she'd had a chance to spend more time with her and ask her questions. More importantly, she wished that she'd found out where on earth she'd been all these years. And if the bright light had meant what she thought it did, could it be that Rosaline had been right all along. That her mother wasn't still on earth at all? Esme shook her head and squeezed her eyes even tighter to banish the very thought.

Yawning and stretching, she opened her eyes and saw her dark blue ceiling painted with stars. She was back in her bed. It had all just been another dream. But it had felt so real!

Esme still desperately wanted to hold onto every word and moment she had spent with her mother. But in the way that dreams do once morning light comes, the memories were already fading. Esme squeezed her eyes tight shut again, trying to force herself back to sleep in the hope she could dream and get back into the gondola with her mother. But it was no use. Her body and mind were awake now and only the final words that her mother had spoken were left echoing in her head:

"If it could only be like this always – always Summer,"

She recognized the phrase from her mother's favourite book, Brideshead Revisited. But she knew when she told Summer and her friends they'd tell her not to read too much into it because it was just another dream.

She stretched again and eased herself up onto her elbows. Her bedroom was just as she'd left it before going to the library the morning before. Eddie, Violet and Aloysius were all sitting in their usual positions on her bed. Her looking glass was hanging from the back of the door, and the Bridge of Sighs painting was at the foot of her bed. And it was definitely the one in Oxford, not Venice!

With everything as it should be she was about to swing her legs out of bed and get ready for the day. Until she spotted something in the corner of her eye that she knew for a fact hadn't been there earlier. The sight of it instantly made the hairs stand up on the back of her neck. Poking out from underneath Aloyisius was something she was certain she'd seen the back of: the corner of a cream envelope. Snatching it from under the bear and seeing her name written in the now familiar writing, she felt like her stomach was filling with cold water. Then turning it over and tearing open the red wax seal she pulled out a plain white card and read its simple message:

> "To find your very oldest friend
>
> Go where Summer never ends."

## Chapter 21 - Summer

Esme was out of breath and her heart was pounding by the time she got to Riverside Cottage. She'd taken a crowded bus from the High Street to the quaint market town of Abingdon, then ran fifteen minutes, not stopping until she could hear her boots crunching along the gravel driveway. She could see Harold reading The Telegraph in the orangery, wearing a red smoking jacket and a captain's hat, with Primrose parked in full view as proud as a daffodil in the morning sun.

She heard the familiar bars of Vivaldi as she rang the doorbell, followed by Hyacinth's sweet voice calling "I'll get it" over the soothing harmonies of choristers on Radio 4.

Seconds later Mrs Hayes appeared in the doorway like an elegant pastel powder puff, wearing a lilac cashmere cardigan with tiny pearl buttons. Her hair was piled in a messy bun on her crown, with streaks of flour across her forehead.

"Oh Esme!" she cried, stretching her arms out to reveal white powdery palms.

"How lovely to see you darling. Now don't look at me, I'm afraid I'm a bit of a mess," she flustered, wiping a loose strand of hair from her face and leaving sticky residue in its place. Her warm maternal smile was quickly replaced by a troubled frown.

"My goodness, you're all pink and out of puff dear. Are you alright darling? Is everything ok?"

"Oh yes thank you Mrs Hayes," Esme gabbled breathlessly, as politely as she possibly could.

"There's really nothing to worry about. Just here to see Summer if that's ok?"

"Well of course dear. She's out in the garden with Daisy and Charles. Come through dear, come through."

Hyacinth wrapped a feather soft arm around Esme's shoulder, and walked her through the hall, which smelt of freshly baked bread, onto a sun drenched patio.

"Summer darling, look who's here to see you!" Hyacinth chirruped across the garden with a theatrical wave to her daughter from the top of the steps.

Summer had her hair in plaits wrapped across her head and was sitting on a long swing hanging from an old oak tree. Her little sister Daisy was playing shop with her dolls on a blanket, along with their dog Charles, dressed in one of their bonnets. His face was as downcast as Summer's was delighted.

"Brains!" she yelled, leaping off her swing, which swung back and forth like a pendulum behind her.

"Am I glad to see you," she added, throwing herself at Esme and wrapping her arms tightly around her neck.

"If I hear 'Twinkle Twinkle Little Shop' one more time I. Will. Scream! Now to what do I owe the pleasure?"

She linked her army firmly through her friend's and ushered her towards a white garden bench by the river.

"Well I know you said it was probably nothing," Esme said sheepishly, taking a seat in the shade of the willow tree.

"But I've had another of those dreams, you know? And another one of those cards. And this one mentions... you."

"*Stop!*" blurted Summer, sitting down, with eyes as wide and blue as the river.

"Ok this is officially getting out of hand now. Well let me see, let me see," she spluttered, gesturing for Esme to open her satchel by making rapid circles with her hand. Esme reached inside, took the envelope out, then placed it into Summer's outstretched palm. She slid the card out and read its words aloud:

"To find your very oldest friend.
Go where Summer never ends."

"Well is that it?" Summer asked, sounding thoroughly nonplussed, before turning it over to see if she could find anything more juicy.

"Well I think I'll hold off on calling my lawyers," she chortled, rolling her eyes.

"But I *am* your oldest friend," she added with a satisfied grin.

"But that's the thing," Esme whispered cagily.

"I don't think that part is about you. You see I had one of my dreams..."

Summer let out an agonized groan.

"No hear me out!" Esme went on hastily.

"I had another dream about Mum, and she told me I used to call her my 'very first friend'. And then the very next morning *that*… was on my bed, under the teddy bear.."

Summer mouthed "Stop" again, but this time no sound came out.

"Ok," she went on, shuffling in her seat to get seriously focussed.

"This is all getting seriously creepy now. So someone is saying your oldest friend, or your Mum as you say, is somewhere Summer never ends?"

"Exactly," said Esme.

"Which is why I came here."

"Well don't look at me!" Summer exclaimed.

"I haven't been hiding your mother in the bushes at Riverside Cottage!"

A loud rustle in the undergrowth made them both jump and shout "Oh my God!" followed by a screeching peacock bolting out, manically flapping his white feathers.

"For God's sake Aristotle!" Summer screamed at the bird.

"*How* many times do I have to tell you not to creep up on me like that!?"

The peacock casually fanned his white plume then turned his back on them, leaving Summer muttering "so arrogant," under her breath.

"My God. We're all going to end up going stark raving bonkers at this rate," she grumbled.

"Right. I've had enough. I am going to get to the bottom of this."

She squeezed her eyes shut and mouthed "Where does Summer never end?" over and over. Until her eyes pinged open, and she shouted:

"Got it!"

Then she grabbed Esme by the hand, and dragged her up the garden and through the house into the orangery.

Harold Hayes was sitting in a large wicker chair above a glass coffee table, surrounded by an array of oversized potted palms. His head was still in The Telegraph as he tapped his slippered foot to a particularly vibrant section of Handel's Messiah.

"Emergency Daddy!" Summer cried, pulling his newspaper down to reveal his bespectacled face and captain's hat.

"What's all this?" he spluttered, all of a fluster, placing his hand on his hat as if to steady the ship.

"I need you to do us a *humongous* favour. I need you to drive Brains and I to her old house in Summertown, and we need to pick up Bambi and Froodle on the way. Somebody there knows something about Brains' Mum."

"*Summer Town*," Esme repeated the words slowly and quietly.

"The town where it's always Summer. Of course," she went on, wondering why on earth she hadn't thought of it sooner.

"I told you you're not the only one with brains, Brains," said Summer, grinning angelically in a stream of sunshine pouring through the roof. Harold's face was still bemused:

"But what makes you…?"

"No time to tell you now Daddy. We'll fill you in once we're in Primrose."

"Right you are," he barked, his military persona rapidly restored. He folded his newspaper neatly on the coffee table then stood up bolt straight.

"If it's an all hands on deck situation, then I'm your man. Now follow me to the bridge."

He marched to the hallway, stepped out of his slippers and slid his pyjamed legs into wellingtons. Then he tightened the cord of his smoking jacket with intent, and marched out the door to his beloved motor car, with the girls hot on his heels.

After cruising through a sunlit Oxfordshire for thirty minutes, Primrose pulled up outside an overgrown garden with a leaning 'For Sale' sign in front of a large detached house. Esme, Freddy and Priya were huddled in the back seat with Summer and her Dad at the front.

"And we're going in… there?" murmured Freddy, gazing up at a roof of missing tiles and burgeoning buddleia.

"Yep. That's the plan…," Summer replied, eyeing the mucky magnolia walls crawling with ivy, having second thoughts herself.

"Come along then," said Priya, jumping out of the back and

putting her hands on her hips to take a proper look.

"We haven't come all this way for nothing."

"Now are you guys absolutely sure?" Esme asked earnestly, as she slid out of the car to join the others. It felt peculiar being so close to her old home: with its trailing roses now smothering the door and little roofs above the upstairs windows which she thought gave it eyes and a happy face.

"I don't want anybody doing anything they're not comfortable with."

"Of course!" the others chimed in unison a little over zealously. Summer hopped out of the passenger seat and wrapped her arm firmly around Esme.

"Look, what are friends for?" she said reassuringly.

"And I'll just be right here keeping an eye on Primrose," said Harold.

"But any sign of trouble and you lot just holler, do you hear? I'll be in there faster than you can say Scuttlebutt!" he added, putting his fingers to his hat in a quick salute.

"Aye aye captain," said Summer, saluting back.

"Right, what are we waiting for? Let's get in and find out what on earth this has all been about!"

Summer pushed a wooden gate, which let out an un-oiled creak. Then they all crept under an archway of untamed honeysuckle and up a mossy pathway towards the front door.

# Chapter 22 - The Bird Cage

Esme could still remember the day her father painted the door of their house a vibrant peach. Her mother had always said the previous door, with its drab oak surface, lacked character and wasn't suited to people with wild imaginations. Her father waited until she was away at Avaley Hall, before choosing a shade he said was as dynamic as she was. Sienna had been as delighted by the surprise as she was the colour, certain its warmth and zest would draw good energy into the home. It made Esme smile to see that, despite the wear and tear on the rest of the house, Andrew's hardy gloss was still going strong.

"So how are we going to get in?" asked Freddy, ever impatient, pushing and kicking the door as hard as he could.

"It's locked and it isn't shifting."

Summer was on her tiptoes looking through a bay window, while Priya peered through the letterbox.

"Follow me," said Esme assertively, walking past the house, then up a narrow pathway battling with a rampant privet hedge. The others followed her to the back of the house, to find a lawn swamped by tall grasses and fluffy dandelion heads, with beds obscured by weeds either side. An untouched orchard, heaving with apples and pears, flourished at the end next to a sprawling silver birch. While a shed, which was once pretty and cream, was now brown and broken down in between. Spotting a rusty trowel sticking out of a terracotta flower pot, Esme grabbed it and made for the large tree. Stamping down a flat patch of grass near its base, she started digging on her hands and knees, until she hit a solid surface.

"Found it," she said triumphantly, beaming up at Summer who was now standing at her side. She hastily knelt down beside her, helping clear the soil away with her hands. She could just make out a wooden surface, with patchy remnants of a sun and moon.

"It's where Dad and I would bury our treasure," Esme went on proudly, tugging at the box to loosen it, until it eventually popped right out. Then, using the edge of her trowel, she carefully leavered it open. Summer peered in to find a rusty jumble of chains, faded beads, broken seashells and a small photograph which had gotten so damp it was almost indecipherable.

"Lovely...," she said blandly.

"No wait," urged Esme, fishing around inside, before drawing out a long chain with a silver feather, a key and a disk engraved with an S.

"S for Sienna," she said, beaming at it.

"And also, for Spare!" she went on, wiggling it in front of Summer's nose, before pushing herself up and running back down the side of the house.

Moments later four friends were standing on a chipped checkerboard floor, which was once the foundation of an immaculate Victorian hallway. An elegant white bannister swirling up from it had lost its shine, while a nearby grandfather clock and piano hid under dust sheets. Though Andrew had made a little money from renting the house out, in recent years it had mostly stood empty and unloved. Esme ran her fingers over the dainty cornflower wallpaper her mother had been so beguiled with when she'd uncovered it in the attic. Despite the fact that it was yellowing around the edges it still gave her a warm glow.

"My goodness. It's all flooding back," said Priya, gazing down from an antique lamp hung from a lofty ceiling with a pendulous dome of textured glass.

"I can just picture us sliding down those stairs when we were little and your Mum playing ragtime tunes underneath."

"Speaking of whom," Freddy interrupted, tapping his foot restlessly on the monochrome floor.

"Where are we planning to begin our hunt?"

Esme was staring into an ornate French mirror decorated with a wreath of golden vines. She could still remember how her mother would pause here to check her outfit before heading to parties. The image brought her scent, a delicate mix of rose and patchouli, back to her.

"She's close by," she said under her breath.

"I can just feel it."

Priya was standing at the bottom of the stairs dangling a silver chain with an amethyst shaved to a point out in front of her. It was steadily swinging back and forth.

"Come… this way," she said quietly, before softly walking up the stairs. The others followed her up to a landing papered in tiny tulips, with four doorways. Esme could remember her mother's expressionist oils of wildflower meadows, where rectangles of paper were now less faded. Watching as the others disappeared into doorways, she walked into the remaining room, which was sparse with a single bed frame and a large concealed object below the window. She walked towards it and carefully pulled away a dust sheet.

"He's still here," she whispered, running her hand across the crimson saddle of the rocking horse she'd last seen in her mother's nursery. She closed her eyes and smelled the wax she used to polish him until he was as smooth as silk, sensing her mother's presence once again. Then she started as the door burst open with Summer sounding like an army cadet:

"Well I've checked the master and Froodle and Bambi did the others. They're pretty much empty aside from basic furnishings. Where next?"

"This way," Priya's voice, so calm by comparison, was calling them back onto the landing. She was standing above her amethyst which was now moving in small circles.

"There's something here," she said confidently, as the others gathered around. They stared at the crystal, then down to a shabby carpet covered in a beige oriental rug.

"You're not saying we need to rip up the floorboards are you?" Freddy asked, staring at his perfect fingernails in alarm.

"Maaaybe," Priya replied slowly, "Unless…"

The others followed as she raised her eyes to the ceiling, and the amethyst started making large pendulous swings.

"The attic?" Esme asked warily. Since she was still small when she and her father had left the house, she'd never been up there.

"Well we've checked everywhere else," said Summer matter of

factly.

"And the crystal's swinging right below the hatch. Is there a ladder?" she asked, looking at Esme.

"I'm not sure… it's been so long…." she replied.

"I think I can remember Dad pulling one down from inside the loft."

"That's easy then," said Summer.

"Just wait right here."

She ran down the stairs, rapidly reappearing with a washing line prop from the garden.

"Stand back," she said dramatically, before hitting the hatch three times with loud thuds until it swung open, revealing the lower rungs of a ladder. She carefully leavered the prop through the bottom and steadily pulled it down.

"Ta dah," she said proudly, thoroughly delighted with her work.

"So who's going up first then?" she added, eyeing them all enthusiastically, though secretly itching to get up there first. The others glanced at one another nervously.

"Never mind," she added with affected martyrdom.

"Apparently I just have to do everything around here."

Already amped up, she climbed the ladder as agilely as a squirrel up a tree, until the soles of her trainers disappeared into the attic. The three friends kept their eyes fixed firmly on the hatch, as Summer's footsteps began slowly echoing around the roof, followed by the distant sound of her voice:

"Guys... you are never going to believe what's up here. I have literally never seen anything like this place. It's like some sort of twisted paradise. And it's so much bigger than I was expecting. So much light and all of this greenery."

Hearing her footsteps echoing again, wondering if this was just another one of Summer's practical jokes, the others glanced at one another looking puzzled.

"Seriously you lot, hurry up. You have got to see this," she went on.

One by one the friends climbed the ladder, hearing the wonder and gasps of those ahead. Until they were all nestled within a jungle of green in an attic mysteriously more like a glass house. The walls were tall with arched windows at each end which could have been straight from a cathedral. Iron candelabras stood like black widows weeping with wax at either side. And a leaded glass ceiling with decorative panes curved to a point overhead. But the most extraordinary sight was the exotic foliage bursting from pots and hanging from the ceiling.

"What on earth is all of this?" Esme said, running her fingers through a stream of golden ivy spilling from a bird cage hung from above. There were potted palms which soared to the ceiling with giant leaves of green and gold; olive trees with silver trunks and shimmering branches; topiary trees twisting like corkscrews; spider plants spilling from pillars; and a myriad of hanging plants cascading from decorative bird cages.

"It's just like a Victorian Conservatory," Esme went on in wonder.

"But how can this possibly be our old attic?"

"Well it's certainly different, I'll give it that," said Summer, standing in a large golden circle painted in the middle of the floor with her arms folded.

"Magical even...," she went on, running her toe across a twelve point star with strange symbols painted within, eyeing it suspiciously.

"But I'm not buying it. It just doesn't make any sense. I mean how can there possibly be windows and a glass ceiling when the roof just looks so ordinary from the outside."

Priya wandered towards them with her hands in her pockets and a blissed-out face upturned.

"Well it's the loveliest place I've ever seen," she said, flickering her eyelashes in the glow from above.

"But I've got to agree with Summer. It can't be real. There has to be some sort of an illusion."

Esme slowly turned in the circle on the floor, basking in the forest of green surrounding her, wondering if she might be dreaming again. Their house in Summertown had always felt special but nothing could possibly have prepared her for this. She spotted Freddy kneeling beneath a window at the end of the room.

"Look," he said, calling Esme over, and pointing to a variety of test tubes and terrariums on the floor.

"It seems like some sort of alchemy's been going on in here. There's even more of this crazy plant stuff being propagated."

Esme crouched down and peered into a miniature glass house

by his side. It contained a twisted bonsai tree bearing golden fruit that looked like tiny jelly beans. Freddy lifted a demijohn sprouting seedlings with a wooden marker reading "black lilies", and mumbled "seriously weird" to himself.

"Whatever next...," Esme said, spotting her reflection in the window, with a wilderness of vegetation flourishing in the background. She slowly made her way back across the room, beneath frothy foliage pouring from bird cages and darkened creepers climbing the walls. Towards the end of the room, she spotted something she recognized.

"It's Mum's desk!" she exclaimed, rushing over to a delicately inlaid mahogany table with a leather surface and three narrow drawers.

"She used to write her novels on it in her garden shed," she explained to Summer who was already leafing through a large leather bound book of pressed flowers.

"But whose are all these things?" she added, pointing towards a huddle of antique bell jars with scarlet cushions displaying an array of curios. There was a crow with feathers as sleek as petrol, butterflies shimmering on lofty pins and even a tiny white rabbit with flawless fur and two perfect heads.

"What the hell...?" said Esme staring back into its four shiny black eyes. Priya had joined them and was picking up paperweights, holding them up to the light. Glass bubbles filled with flowers and frozen dragonflies twisted before her, with the light shooting through them casting rainbows across the desk. Finally she came to a silver paperweight, as round and flat as an ice puck. A five point star was finely etched on its surface surrounded by letters, numbers and symbols.

"A pentagram," she murmured, placing it on her outstretched

palm.

"Someone who dabbles in magic must have been in here."

"Why, what's a pentagram?" Esme asked tentatively.

"Well that really depends on whose it is," Priya replied, cupping it in her hands so Esme could see.

"For some it's a sign of life. You see the five points of the star represent air, fire, water, earth and spirit. Those who see it that way use it for protection against evil."

Esme nodded as she lifted the pentagram and studied its strange markings. The star's symbols certainly looked curious with its tiny daggers and astrological signs.

"And what else?" she asked.

"Well," Priya went on, lowering her voice.

"If it should happen to fall into the wrong hands it could be dangerous. There are those who use it for witchcraft, sorcery and black magic. Some even call it the Devil's Trap!"

Esme spotted two small eyes staring up from the top of the star, and promptly dropped it back onto the desk.

"But fortunately for us we're only surrounded by white witches. Goddess of the highest order," Priya added, giving her a reassuring squeeze.

"Exactly," Summer agreed, glancing furtively at Priya before continuing.

"But I do think you ought to look at this."

She was holding the pressed flower book open in front of Esme, pointing to a list of Latin plant names. They were written in beautiful black font to correspond with flowers on the opposite page.

"The writing," said Esme darkly, casting her eyes over the swirling italics.

"It's exactly like the writing on the cards and envelopes," she added with a shudder.

Summer nodded.

"I know. But at least it means we're getting closer," she reassured, before closing the book, placing it back on the desk with the pentagram on top for safe keeping. Esme's eyes shifted across to a pile of hardback novels, topped with a crimson Tess of the D'urbervilles.

"These were Mum's too," she said, tracing her fingers over the embossed cover, before spotting another book she recognised.

"It can't be…" she said, grabbing it from the pile, feeling her heart rate quicken. The others watched as she pulled out a cream book which was faded and worn with a swirling grey crest on its cover.

"How on earth did this get here? Look. It's the first edition of Brideshead Revisited. And it looks exactly the same as the one from my dream. The one Dad gave to Mum on their wedding morning."

Esme had tried to keep her dreams of her Mum alive in her mind for as long as she could. But while some details had faded, the book and the fact she already knew what it looked like had remained as a strange anomaly.

"You don't think…?" Summer blurted, before shaking her head, instantly regretting the thought.

"That Dad did all of this?" Esme snapped.

"That's what you were going to say isn't it?"

A loud creak from a rusty hinge made the girls turn around before Summer could reply.

"Look at this."

Freddy was on his hands and knees rifling through the contents of an old wooden trunk that had been hidden beneath a weeping cherry blossom by the wall. He started lifting evening dresses out one by one: a pink chiffon strapless, followed by a lilac taffeta ball gown, then a black satin full-length, placing them neatly in a pile next to him. Esme sat down beside him, pulling out long strings of pearls and smart pairs of heels.

"It's all her stuff," she said bleakly, before looking at Freddy, who was busy admiring a polka dot tea dress. Quickly refocusing, he leaned into the bottom of the trunk and pulled out a long white cardboard box, before gently handing it to Esme. She hesitantly took it from him, her mind reeling with its potential contents. The others gathered around as she silently opened it, then watched as her face flooded with confusion. Inside the box was an ivory silk dress, a long lace veil and a dried bouquet of white flowers. They all looked precisely as she remembered them in her dream.

"And your Dad is fond of his telescope isn't he?" Freddy said apologetically, nodding to the glass ceiling.

"But why on earth would my Dad of all people send me the notes?" Esme spluttered. She thought about how Aloysius had mysteriously ended up back on her bed with another card after she'd left him out for her father. Her blood instantly started to pound inside her head.

"I mean how could he possibly do that to me? What kind of a sick joke has he been playing? And does this mean that Rosaline was right? Did he actually know about Mum all along? I mean for god sake. It's like a bloody shrine in here!"

She pushed herself to her feet and started pacing around the room. Of all the people who could have possibly betrayed her, how could it have been her Dad all along. The kind, decent and dependable Professor Drake, who went out of his way to make time for everyone and always did the right thing. She wanted to believe that they were all mistaken, but who else would possibly have the access or inclination to do something like this? Within a matter of minutes, and with this single revelation, Esme's faith in the world had been indelibly crushed. She heard Dougal's haughty voice warning her that it only takes one wrong move for the house of cards to fall down, and felt a sting, like she was the joker of the pack. Unable to contain her pain any longer she stormed over to the desk, swiping its contents to the floor. Then she fell to her knees, with her shoulders heaving with heavy sobs. Priya instantly rushed over and started stroking her hair, while Freddy sheepishly replaced the contents of the trunk, thinking perhaps he should have kept them to himself. Summer waited a moment or two before speaking.

"Guys," she said quietly.

"I don't mean to alarm you, but I think things may have just gotten even more weird."

Her voice was coming from behind a shimmering cascade of lilac foliage.

"Oh what now...?" Esme groaned, pressing the heels of her palms into her eyes

"Come on," said Priya softly, supporting her by the elbows and helping her up. She put her arm around her waist, leading her across the golden circle on the floor towards the sound of Summer's voice. Freddy quietly closed the trunk and followed. One by one, they made their way beneath a waterfall of wisteria hanging from above. They found Summer standing next to a veil of thin white gauze, hovering like a ghost.

"I thought I heard something hidden in here you see," she explained, turning to face the mysterious fabric then swooping down and carefully lifting it with both hands. She threw it back and smoothed it down, just as a groom would tenderly unveil a bride. Beneath it was an ornate golden birdcage on a stand carved with twisting vines. The friends leaned in and gazed between the bars, as if its contents were an unseen Monet, letting out gasps of amazement.

"Is it real?" Esme asked through sniffles, with her face still moist with tears.

"Yeah I think so. I heard it making a noise," Summer whispered, keeping her voice low so as not to startle the cage's inhabitant.

"Look, its eyes are moving and its chest is breathing. I'd say that it's very much real."

Inside the cage was a beautiful white bird on a swing. Its wings and tail were long and softly feathered, with sparkles of gold at their tips. A silvery breastplate shone up to its beak, which was mirrored in gold right up to its crown. And an angel's breath fountain of white plumed from its head above eyes that were small and green. As if wishing to prove its sentience the bird opened its tiny beak and made a soft trilling noise as pure as a shower of tiny diamonds.

"Simply exquisite," Freddy sighed, stroking his chin like a philosopher, in an enraptured state of awe.

"But it's so sad," Priya said, blinking back at the bird, with eyes as earnest as an injured fawn.

"I wonder how long it's been stuck in that tiny cage? Poor little innocent thing. Look at its lovely wings. They're so beautiful and so long. It really needs to be set free."

Priya's lithe fingers had already started pressing and feeling around the birdcage, trying to find a door or a catch to loosen. Just as she was opening her mouth to speak again, the room fell dark.

"Errrr guys. What's going on?" said Summer, sounding slightly more alarmed than she'd wished to let on.

But before anyone had a chance to respond a venomous voice growled a sinister warning from within.

## Chapter 23 - The Dark Stranger

"Get out!"

Just two cautionary words were dealt before the room fell silent again, bar the sound of the friends' hearts pounding in their ears.

"What do we do?" Freddy mouthed, trying not to fidget, with eyes full of fear. Priya took a deep breath, then calmly parted the wall of wisteria. The daylight had mysteriously vanished, but something new had appeared: the silhouette of a cloaked figure in front of an arched window. Freddy started tapping his toe which made Summer stamp on top of it, glowering at him with her finger on her lips. Esme quietly cleared her throat and swallowed.

"Who's there?" she called out hesitantly, trying her best to keep her voice measured and calm. This was her house after all and she had no intention of being intimidated. Despite the fact her palms were clammy and she could feel a vein in her temple throbbing with anxiety.

There was a whoosh as the candelabras ignited with flames, which made Summer grip onto Freddy's arm and Freddy bite his fist. Softly illuminated between them was a small woman clothed in a fitted black dress, which swept around her ankles and buttoned high up her neck. Her hair was twisted up into a chignon, held in place with three delicate green gems. A striking emerald and diamond eye pinned to her chest made everyone feel watched. Nobody had heard her enter and the hatch was closed. She lifted her arms beneath her cloak to enhance her stature and glared at them like a crow.

"None of you have any business being in here," she rasped furiously.

So get out…Now!"

She threw her arms up like bat wings, before brandishing a fist adorned with onyx and ruby rings. Freddy quickly made a cross over his body, kissed the thumbs of his praying hands and pressed them to his forehead. It was clammy with tiny beads of perspiration. Esme's face was flushed with fury and her mouth as dry as desert sand. But without flinching, she calmly walked towards the woman until she was standing square on to her.

"You," she said, folding her arms across her chest assuredly, her voice as cool and heavy as a stone.

"I should have known it was you all along."

Hetty, looking far more put together than Esme had ever seen her, was staring back with eyes shimmering like amethyst clusters in the candlelight.

"Now now. Hetty only wants to help you," she chided. Her voice sounded slithery and insincere. She was inching towards Esme so smoothly she appeared to be floating. Esme stared her dead in the eye, determined to stand her ground. As the woman drew closer she stretched her long, gnarled fingers out to stroke her hair. Esme went to smack them away but, fast as lightning, Hetty grabbed her wrist, leering towards her so their faces were almost touching.

"Now you listen to me missy," she hissed through breath that smelled like rotting onions.

"It's time that you respect your elders. Age and wisdom come before beauty, you know. And it's beauty that I am trying to protect you from. Trust me when I say it's not safe for you here."

She spun Esme around, pulling her arm up behind her back, then started pushing her towards the circle in the centre of the floor. Summer stepped forward to intervene but Priya cautiously pulled her back.

"Now come along," Hetty went on blithely, putting her weight into Esme's struggling body. Attempting a more persuasive tone she went on.

"We must work as a team. If we turn this magic circle into a sacred space it will keep us both safe. Like goddesses together you see."

Hetty grabbed Esme's shoulders and spun her around so they were standing eye to eye. Her calloused fingers grabbed her arms so tight it made her wince and her face was luminous with triumph.

"But we mustn't delay. He'll be here soon."

"What the hell are you talking about you mad woman?" Esme moaned, trying to free herself from the shackle she was in.

"I want no more of you and this cruel game. It's over Hetty!"

She swung her arms up, tugging them open with such force that Hetty's hands flew apart like a jack in a box. She instantly threw them over her head, cowering dramatically, just like she'd done at the riverside. But this time Esme wasn't prepared to offer sympathy.

"Now tell me what you know about my mother," she demanded, pointing her finger.

"Where the hell is she? And how did you get in here, and find all of her things?"

Esme glared at Hetty crouched on her knees, quivering and whimpering.

"And to think you even made me suspect my father could be behind this circus," she went on, her voice breathless and impassioned.

"Well I'm not your performing monkey Hetty. And I want no more to do with this twisted side show. Just tell me what happened to my Mum. Then get the hell out of my life!"

A mysterious light had begun to shine on Hetty's face, making her shield her eyes.

"It's too late," Hetty whined like a spoiled child.

"Hetty tried to warn you. But it's too late," she insisted, shrinking further from the light.

"What's too late?" Esme asked irritably, confused by the woman's change in demeanour, but wildly suspicious of her motive.

"You're not making any sense Hetty. This is just another one of your stupid stunts."

Esme saw Hetty's tiny body, crumpled in a pool of light, and looked up to see where it was coming from. A mysterious beam was flooding through the ceiling, as clear as a spot light. Hetty started shuffling backwards with her eyes fixed on the intensifying pool of light. Pushing herself to her feet, and gathering up her dress, she stared terror-stricken at Esme and screamed:

"He's here!"

She ran away like a startled animal, until the tip of her cape vanished into a swathe of green. Esme could see the light on the floor getting brighter and brighter.

"Errrr... what's happening?" asked Freddy, popping up from behind a voluminous brass pot, where he'd been hiding. He visibly shuddered as the flames on the candelabras all went out.

"Ok, now this is officially getting weird," he mumbled, shaking his head as black smoke coiled up from their shouldering wicks.

"I think this is probably the right time to call in the Admiral. Don't you?" he added, tilting his head, like it was a blatant understatement. Summer was already kneeling at the hatch, trying to prise it open with her fingernails.

"It's no good, it won't budge," she moaned, thumping it with her fist, thoroughly exasperated. She stood up and stamped on it with all her might. Esme could see the hanging birdcages beginning to sway and felt the air getting cooler. The wind was starting to whistle, with dust swirling above the spotlight like a miniature hurricane.

"Hetty, where the hell are you?" Esme cried, running to where she'd disappeared and parting a wall of paddle shaped leaves. She was nowhere to be seen.

"This isn't funny. Come out and open the hatch so that we can get out... immediately!" she yelled, hearing her voice echoing off the ceiling. Esme could now feel the force of the twister. The light appeared to be spinning with it, as it started picking up leaves and petals from the floor. Esme looked around for the others but they were nowhere to be seen. As the twister started to grow taller and wider Esme sensed something menacing lurking within, with a kaleidoscope of light now swirling around it. Until eventually the light flashed so bright that it flooded the room, causing Esme to scream and squeeze her eyes shut, before collapsing to the floor.

Feeling the same sensation in the pit of her stomach as when she'd plunged down the well and been sucked through the painting, Esme instinctively knew she was about to meet her antagonist. Who or what that might appear as she shuddered to find out. Slowly opening her eyes to find the conservatory now shrouded in darkness, she could still make out the sinister shape of the dark creature from within the twister. As she inched away, the candelabras swiftly ignited and her tormentor was finally revealed.

A head of thick silver hair was slicked back above the upright collar of a black velvet cloak with a rich sweeping cape. Its outline was majestic but its existence menacing. *The Dark Stranger, my enigmatic puppet master,* Esme thought, glancing to see if Hetty was around, wishing she'd heeded her advice. The figure started to raise its arms beneath the cloak, revealing golden threads at the edges, before gently pivoting around like a sinister doll on a jewellery box. Esme lowered her eyes, blowing slowly through pursed lips as she prepared to meet her persecutor. Finally. She looked up.

"It was you?"

Esme uttered three short words, as her heart began to sink, bewildered by the face before her.

"You did all of this?"

There was no answer. Just two small eyes staring calmly back at her.

"But how did you get in? And how could you do this to me... and Dad? You're not a stranger. I mean for all those years. You were more than just a friend to us, you were..."

Dougal was standing in the centre of the magic circle looking more self possessed than Esme had ever seen him.

"Family?" rasped a familiar voice. Hetty had emerged from her hideaway. Her tiny body looked frail against the gothic window.

"He's not your family dear. And how I wish that he was never mine. From the moment I gave birth to him he was like a malevolent imposter. Slight of spirit and black of heart. Dougal was the designation he brought upon himself. It's an ancient name cultivated in my Celtic roots, with a meaning as literal as it is antiquated. I named him Dougal, because it means: 'The Dark Stranger'."

"Enough!" Dougal cried like a petulant child, sweeping his cloak towards Hetty with such ferocity it made the candles flicker and the old woman cower in terror.

"How dare you speak of me like that. When it was your twisted logic and bitter soul that made me this way. Casting your love charms, forcing me to cherish women. *You* caused all of this!" he roared, surging towards Hetty then hovering above her like a hawk.

"What?" Esme said in astonishment. Whispers of Hetty's days as a dancer in Paris and that chance encounter with a film director in the Maison Souquet came flooding back.

"You mean to tell me that you two knew one another. That Dougal's your *son*?"

"Don't!" Hetty cried, covering her ears like she couldn't bear to hear the word.

"That creature is no offspring of mine. I tried to make him good. I tried to make him respect women. But an animal with such a dark heart is incapable of love. That's why I cast the spell on him. I thought I could turn him into a better man. But it went terribly, terribly wrong. Making him dangerous and obsessed with your mother instead."

"Obsessed?" Esme said incredulously. She knew that Dougal had always been fixated on minor details and was nervous about his health. But she never saw his obsessiveness as a threat. Summer, Priya and Freddy had crept around Esme filled with bewilderment and concern.

"Now listen you," Summer said, storming over to Dougal and jabbing him repeatedly in the shoulder. He spun around, with a whip of his cloak and an air of vexation.

"Now I don't know what kind of game you're playing here Donald," she went on, pointing her finger at him.

"Errr I think it's Dougal," Freddy stage whispered, smoothing his hair sheepishly.

"Whatever your name is," she went on, folding her arms.

"It could be Batman for all I care! But you listen to me. This isn't some crazy fancy dress party and this isn't your house. So just tell Brains what you know about her Mum. Then get yourself and all of your creepy plants out of here for good!"

"What makes you think I know anything about that?" Dougal asked provocatively, twisting his mouth into a wry smile.

"Errr well the weird notes and Esme's trippy dreams for a start…"

"Now come along Esmeralda," Dougal went on, spinning gracefully on his heel before drifting eerily towards Esme.

"You know that there's no truth in dreams, and you could save yourself a world of trouble by not bothering to look for any."

Esme felt the hairs stand up on the back of her neck, just as they had when she thought she was being watched in the lodge. It all made complete sense now. The fleeting sight of a cloak at the lodge, the use of her full name Esmeralda, Dougal sitting on top of the barge telling her not to read into dreams. When all the time he knew exactly how cruelly she was being played, almost to breaking point, not knowing who to trust. Without warning she flew towards Dougal in a rage, beating his chest with her fists, sobbing uncontrollably.

"Why??? Why did you do this to us? And what have you done with her? She's my Mum, I need her!"

Everyone had fallen silent in the conservatory, bar the sound of Esme's cries and the distant chirp of the bird in the cage.

"Just tell me where she is Dougal," she pleaded desperately.

"I've played your game and now I'm at the end of this ridiculous sham. Now you have to play your part."

The bird's chirping was getting louder and louder with Dougal, shooting furtive looks in its direction. Then it broke into a crystal clear melody, with a voice as pure as its feathers.

"That blasted parrot!" Dougal shouted, watching tensely as Esme, followed by the others, wandered towards its cage. One by one they formed an arc around the bird, gazing as its pretty beak and emerald eyes opened and closed. A hauntingly beautiful tune was drifting towards them.

"I know that tune," said Esme, looking misty eyed and mystified.

"It's the Hymnus Eucharisticus. The one that the choir sings on May Morning. My Dad never misses it because it reminds him of my Mum. But how can it...?"

The bird continued its sweet song, puffing its silver breast out and singing with all its might, its little green eyes blinking earnestly back at theirs.

"It can't be," said Freddy open mouthed, as a look of realisation followed by horror shot between the friends.

"Is the bird your...?"

"No!!!" Dougal cried out, surging towards them and sweeping his cloak around the cage to conceal it. His eyes looked as alarmed as Esme remembered them when she used to make him jump in the glass houses.

"I wanted to tell you. I needed to tell you. That witch had cast her spell on me so I couldn't control my actions. But week after week, when I saw your father at Perditus Amor, and you at the gardens, the guilt would eat me up. *That's* why I sent the cards and gifts. I just knew I needed to get you here. To explain my grave mistake and give Sienna back to you."

"*LIES!!!*" Hetty screeched as she flew towards Dougal, her grasping hand whipping his cloak back to reveal the bird. Then she turned and pleaded with Esme like an innocent child.

"Can you see it now dear? Hetty did try to warn you. It's not safe for you here. I told you that seeing is believing. So come quick. Follow me."

Dougal's eyes grew wide with fear as Hetty folded her cloak around Esme like a tiny angel wing, ushering her to the other side of the room. Creeping into a darkened den, thick with trailing vines, Esme found herself staring at another white veil hovering like a spirit.

"Look," said Hetty, eyeing her excitedly, before reaching down, whisking the veil away in one surprisingly graceful movement.

"Well… it's just another birdcage," said Esme disappointedly, cocking her head in case she was missing something. She shrugged at Summer and Freddy who had crept in to join her.

"Empty…" rasped Hetty, pointing a bony finger towards the bird cage and then twirling it knowingly at Esme.

"Can't you see it now? You're the double of your mother. Both of you, such rare beauties with your ravishing locks and emerald orbs. The dark one never intended to give Sienna back dear. He wanted *you*!" she rasped, exhaling with relief to have finally revealed her son's twisted plan.

"What?" said Esme in horror.

"You mean all this time? The cards… the teddy… the pendant. It was all just part of Dougal's plan to trap *me*? And I've just been going along with it like a fool?"

"I'm so sorry dear. I tried to tell you," Hetty said softly, her pale eyes full of sorrow. Esme took Hetty gently by the shoulders and stared her seriously in the eye.

"Look Hetty. I'm so sorry for the way I've treated you. I should have listened to you before," she offered sincerely.

"But I *really* need your help now. I came here to get my mother. And I'm not leaving the attic without her. But how can I possibly rescue her and bring her back?"

"Well my dear," Hetty went on sagely.

"Since a dark and selfish heart corrupted my love charm and caused all of this, there's only one conceivable way it can ever be undone."

"And what's that?" Esme asked nervously, picturing a black cauldron bubbling with newts eyes, rabbits feet and bats wings.

"Why the exact opposite my dear. I was drifting by in Asphodel when I spotted you and your friends in that Riverside garden that day. You were like a ring of goddesses. Filled with heavenly joy and bonded by the purest of friendship and love. And that's when I knew I had to find you. Because *you* have the power to overcome The Dark Stranger. By using the one thing he will never have…"

Hetty's eyes were sparkling in a face that had softened in the dusky light. For the very first time Esme caught a glimpse of the beguiling young dancer who once dazzled the audiences in Paris.

"Right then troops," Summer interrupted like an army officer, stepping forward to initiate her military operation.

"So here's the plan. We've left Bambi in charge of Dougal and the bird. Froodle, you grab the pentagram before whatshisface gets it. And Brains, just get in the middle of the circle with Hetty, and *DON'T MOVE*! It's time to bring down this mad house once and for all!"

## Chapter 24 - Tree of Life

Minutes later four friends were sitting on the floor of an enchanting candlelit conservatory, lush with green. A beautiful white bird in a golden cage was chirping delightfully in between. But in spite of its dulcet tones, Summer was frowning and twisting her mouth.

"But I just don't get it…" she said, looking at Priya incredulously.

"I thought the whole reason Dougal got us up here was to trap us."

"I know," Priya agreed with a bemused shrug.

"I mean, I was trying my best to guard him. But he seemed so rattled by what Hetty was about to show Esme that he started muttering to himself. Then he ran off, leaving the bird with me. I just assumed he'd come looking for you lot. But perhaps he hadn't expected to be confronted by so many of us."

Summer narrowed her eyes like a cat.

"Well it all sounds a bit fishy to me," she said, sounding like a cynical copper.

"I don't believe he'd give up his evil plan just like that. Not after all this time and effort. Though you're right. He did seem pretty scared of Hetty."

"Damn right he should be scared," said Freddy furiously.

"I can't believe that creep was lining up another one of his gilded cages to trap madam here. I mean, I know I keep saying you need to attract more male attention, but that's taking things way too far," he said, licking his tongue out at Esme after she punched him in the arm.

"Now now children," Hetty coaxed huskily, shuffling from behind the desk, carrying a leather bound book of spells. It was dark and weathered and as thick as a house brick, with a huge brass clasp.

"To cast my spell auspiciously there must be purity of heart, not drollery and fisticuffs," she scolded like a children's nanny, though tickled pink to be part of the clan.

"Ahhh the heavens are already sending their blessings and good fortune our way," she rasped, raising her eyes to the glass ceiling.

"With the flower moon still in abundance, our sorcery to end this poor creature's incarceration will be all the more potent."

She let out a soft, satisfied cackle.

"Amen to that," said Freddy, with his hands in the air, before seeing Hetty's disapproving glare and dragging them down his cheeks to deadpan his face. The bird let out another one of its cut glass perfect trills, as if she were keen to hurry things along too.

"Now. We must charm the magic circle to work for us rather than against us," Hetty went on, moving around the group surprisingly gracefully, cradling her heavy tome in her spindly arms.

"It's imperative we infuse them with pertinent energy. Magic only works when the intention is clear."

The friends nodded to each other as if this seemed to make sense.

"According to the Grimoire," she said majestically, as she opened her book.

"One must forge a sacred altar of materials denoting the purity of friendship and love. Then blend a wild potion to seal the charm. But it's important we make haste. Before the dark one returns."

Then she floated off in the direction of the terrariums and test tubes nestled below the window.

While Hetty mixed her magic brew the friends followed her instructions, gathering as many symbols of love and friendship as they could find. Esme tied her cerise scarf, gifted from Freddy, in a bow on top of the birdcage, while Summer placed long branches of pink and white apple blossom around them on the ground. Priya cleansed the Brideshead and baptisia pendant of negative energy with the pentagram and placed them all at the base of the cage, along with her amethyst crystal, Esme's birthday watch and Sienna's wedding bouquet. Then they formed a circle around the birdcage, patiently waiting for the spell to commence.

Hetty soon drifted back to them carrying a tiny corked jar, not much bigger than her thumb, along with a small brass bowl.

"Very good my dears. The altar appears to be quite satisfactory," she rasped, with her eyes flashing violet with delight.

"All it requires now is my witches' bottle: a subtle blend of dragon's blood, tiger's eye, rosemary and white feather," she said proudly, holding the tiny bottle up to her eye, before hovering it below a candelabra and sealing it with a drop of wax. She floated forward, placing it with the other items at the base of the cage. Then holding out her brass bowl she began circling the friends.

"Seize a pinch of salt, and then the incantation shall commence. Once you hear my song summoning the gods and goddesses to help us, you must sprinkle it upon the altar then immediately join hands. But please listen carefully. Whatever you do. You must *not* break the circle of protection. Until I tell you that it is safe to do so."

She steadily made her way back to the window, hovering in front of it just as she'd arrived, cradling the spell book open in her arms. Then she closed her eyes and started swaying, humming an old Celtic tune like a mystic mermaid enticing sailors into the sea. On hearing her voice, the friends carefully sprinkled their salt over the objects at the base of the cage, before returning to their circle and clasping one another's hands. With the ring of protection safely secured, Hetty opened her eyes and began to speak in a deep and haunting voice:

"In the name of the Carpundia river goddess.
And Damona's mineral springs.
Seven swans and seven mosses.
Protect from the darkness he brings.
Like the battles of Cathubodua,
And Caturix with all his might,
Seize the strength of Adsagsona,
Charm the heavens to grant their light."

Mesmerised by Hetty's magical incantation, the friends looked up, as a beam of pure white light pierced through the glass ceiling. It reached down to the birdcage, glowing like a pillar to Heaven. Smiling to see it safe and secure, Hetty started to chant again:

"In the name of Loucetios' thunder,
By the light of the Black Moon,
Sirona and Belenus shall heal her,
Bring her back into the room.
With dragon's blood and tiger eye,
Rosemary and feather,
Cernunnos with golden horns,
Bring kindred back together."

The friends watched in awe as the silk scarf started unwinding itself from the top of the birdcage. Then it slowly spiralled up through the glowing beam, mysteriously twisting branches and sprouting leaves until it formed into a beautiful golden tree.

"The Tree of Life," whispered Freddy in amazement, before adding:

"Well I do always buy the best gifts."

The door of the cage silently opened, as the bird fluttered out, spreading its wings and flying up into the boughs of the tree. Hetty gazed up blissfully as it let out an angelic whistle. Then she continued chanting in her slow rhythmic voice:

"Summon the great Morrigan,
Three sisters to set her free.
Brigid and all your wisdom,
Bring her back where she should be.
Winding and weaving never deceiving,
With a love as pure as snow,
Entwined together by roots forever,
It's time to let her go."

Hetty lifted her arms gracefully like wings as the beam of light started to get brighter, reaching through the trunk of the tree and down into the floor. The friends looked on in astonishment as the bird started to grow bigger, gaining limbs and finally lustrous long auburn hair. The light eventually became so bright that the bird and tree appeared to disappear, blanched by its intensity. Until it softly faded back, revealing a beautiful woman encircled within the pillar of light.

"Mum," Esme said softly, gazing at her mother looking as resplendent and lovely as she had in the gondola.

"You brought me home," her mother said, in a voice as sweet as the bird's, as a single tear rolled down her cheek. Priya, Freddy and Summer stared at Sienna in wonder, before smiling at one another with affection. But just as Esme was basking in the adoration in her mother's eyes, a vile and desperate voice cried out from above:

"Sienna, my love. Come back to me!"

Esme spun around to see Dougal, swooping down from the peak of the arched window before landing on the desk with a thunderous crash. Fired up with familial protectiveness she stepped forward, stretching her arms out to shield her mother.

"My love?!" she spat furiously at the dark figure looming over her like a demon of the underworld.

"What do you know about love? You're nothing but a selfish old man!"

"No! The circle of protection!" Hetty wailed desperately.

But it was too late. The beam of light surged down from

the ceiling, striking Esme and Dougal like a bolt of lightning, making them instantly collapse to the floor. Then it crashed through the window with an ear splitting shatter. And one by one the plants started to disappear as the enchanted conservatory softly melted away. Quick as a flash, Hetty shot across the room, cloak billowing, before kneeling over Esme's body and desperately feeling for a pulse.

"Hetty do something!" Priya cried out.

The four friends crouched down feeling helpless, as Hetty gently turned Esme's loose body onto her back, easing her heavy head onto her lap.

"What's happening?" sobbed Summer.

"I mean she'll be ok right?"

The conservatory was swiftly returning to a regular attic with sloping walls held up with thick oak beams. Sienna's writing desk was still at one end with her chest of clothes pushed against the wall. But the friends were too fraught to notice.

"Hetty," Freddy pleaded.

"Say something. Please!"

Hetty seemed lost in a trance, bent over Esme, stroking her face then desperately pressing her fingers to her limp wrist and pallid neck. But it was no use. Agonised by the anguished faces around her, but unable to offer them comfort, Hetty threw back her head, let out a blood curdling wail, before folding her sobbing body over Esme's lifeless one.

# Chapter 25 - Endless Summer

The morning after darkness as black as night had descended upon an ordinary attic in Summertown, the sun arose above the river just like it always did. Despite Hetty's wretched cries, a summer filled with endless days of picnics, punting and parties still followed. Then after nature's alchemist had turned its green into russet gold, a thick blanket of crystal white settled upon the meadow. Until sleepy snowdrops popped their heads above its cover, telling all of creation that morning had broken once again.

It was noon on a cloudless Sunday in July and our star had made its way around the sun for a second time. Christ Church meadow was basking in a haven of sunlight and bliss. The outline of the ancient university buildings was magnificent beyond, their silver steeples and gilded domes glistening in the sky. On the ground the streets were bustling, with tourists roaming and students cycling, their eyes fixed forward with baskets full of books. And a single blackbird atop the tallest building, Magdalen Tower, cried out its sweet song, as it looked down upon a city full of people, glad to be alive.

But one couple moved quietly with their heads bowed as they made their way across Christ Church Meadow. Andrew Drake wrapped his arm around his wife as they drifted from the Cherwell to the memorial gardens on the other side. Silently they turned into an enclosed lawn, beneath the soaring spires and stained glass windows of the college's Grand Hall. Then they paused to admire its perfect flower beds, planted in a circle around a pond, surrounded by old brick walls and soft herbaceous borders.

"Let's do it right here," Andrew said, looking down at the freshly mown grass, encircling the garden, beneath his feet.

"She always loved the Rose Garden. And Summer told me she'd never seen her looking more happy than when they took her to Christ Church's ball on her sixteenth birthday. So this is the perfect place."

Sienna nodded at her husband, then threw a soft grey blanket up by its corners so it caught the air, then floated down to the ground. Andrew placed a picnic hamper on top of it, then they both sat down alongside. Imagining his daughter living life to the full, just behind the garden's walls, Andrew's eyes became misty.

"I'm just going to miss her so much," he said with a sigh, drawing a knee up and resting his chin on it.

"She was such a rock to me all those years that you were away, you know?"

"I know," Sienna replied softly, stroking her husband's arm.

"We're all going to miss her terribly. The way she stepped forward by herself to confront that dreadful creature was so unbelievably brave. I'm just so proud to have had a daughter like that. I literally owe her my life."

Andrew looked lovingly at his wife, smoothed a lock of hair behind her ear then lifted a gold locket, shimmering on her chest. He clicked it open, gazing down at a photograph of his daughter smiling up at him with her beautiful green eyes. Then the pair sat quietly for a moment, before unpacking their picnic in the tranquil surrounds of their secluded paradise.

Meanwhile...

Back on the busier side of Christ Church, a small figure on a bicycle was breezing up the High Street, with her recently chopped red hair tucked neatly behind her ears. Esme

Drake could never understand how people could pass these resplendent buildings with their noses to the ground, when a sight so close to heaven hovered just below the clouds. As she turned at Carfax and cycled down St Aldates, a flock of doves took to the air from the top of Tom Tower. It was a sight which made her heart smile. Then she locked up her bike, marched through decorative wrought iron gates, and down a meandering stone path to the Rose Garden.

Seeing her Mother and Father, reunited in their own private wonderland, was the loveliest sight Esme had ever seen. Andrew was the first to spot his daughter hurrying towards them, with her emerald eyes laughing and her russet bob bouncing around her face. He immediately beamed back, before tapping his watch in mock impatience.

"You're late!" he teased, as she planted a kiss on each of their cheeks before plonking herself down in front of them.

"Still running on Oxford time Dad. Always five minutes late," she joked back, breathless from her bike ride.

"Try telling that to Rupert," he said.

"No time for that!" they both chimed, laughing at the coincidence.

"Actually I went to see Hetty," Esme went on.

"I've been helping her sort that rooftop out of hers. Bought her some big wooden planters and filled them with fresh heather and herbs. She's chuffed."

Hetty and Esme had grown close in the months after the incident in the attic. Hetty had felt the faintest breath after she'd thrown herself on Esme's body in despair. Then she'd used all of the powers she could harness to bring her back, before making daily visits with herbs and potions until she was fully restored. She said it was only the power of the pure love surrounding her which had spared Esme while Dougal had perished.

"What a funny old world she lives in," Esme said, with eyes full of fondness.

"I'm actually quite fascinated by her and look forward to popping over and helping around Asphodel now. She's the most mischievous character, full of incredible stories."

"What a life she's led," agreed Sienna.

"But imagine having a son like Dougal. How on earth did he turn out so terrible? And so powerful. Drawing us both in like that. Even manipulating us through our dreams."

Esme's face became sombre, as she cast her mind back to that dreadful night.

"I know. Hetty told me that after her love charm went wrong, his sorcery became much stronger. And that by planting objects, like the Brideshead Revisited and the baptisia pendant on us, he could control us even more."

Sienna shuddered at the thought.

"And the way he grew all those strange plants for me. Thinking *that* would be enough to make me sing for him, love him even. What a creep," she added.

Andrew's face had turned as grey as the stone walls, and he was clenching his fists so tight, his knuckles had gone translucent.

"That duplicitous old swine," he muttered, with a venom Esme had rarely witnessed in him.

"The sheer gall of him coming to our home every week. After he'd stolen my wife and ruined our lives. Why if I could just…"

Seeing his temper rising, Sienna placed her hand on his shoulder and looked him calmly in the eyes.

"Come on now Drew," she soothed, gently squeezing his tight muscles.

"It's over. He's gone now. There's no point in dwelling on the past. We have one another now, that's all that matters. Let's just focus on the future."

At the word "future" a look of recognition flickered between the couple. Glancing at Sienna, Andrew said:

"Is now the right time to do it?"

Sienna smiled and nodded back with her steady gaze.

"What's going on?" asked Esme, unnerved by their sudden change of demeanour.

"Now it's nothing to worry about Petal," Andrew said softly, as he reached into the picnic hamper.

"It's just that something arrived for you in the post this morning."

Esme looked nervously towards her Mum and Dad as he passed her an envelope. She plucked it tentatively from his hand, as her stomach did an habitual flip. Then she quickly tore it open, unfolded a letter and silently read its contents. Then with her eyes still firmly fixed on the paper, she quietly said under her breath:

"I got in."

Then she took a deep breath and slowly read the letter aloud:

"We are writing to confirm that you have been awarded a place to study at Paris College of Art."

She read it silently over a couple more times before searching her father's face for a reaction:

"That means I'm going to..."

"France," he replied quietly, with his eyes to the ground, trying to register the news himself. Then with tears of joy welling in his eyes he looked up and said:

"*My* daughter is going to be an artist. In Paris!" with his Yorkshire accent getting thicker, as it tended to when he was either elated or inebriated.

"That is absolutely bloody brilliant!"

Andrew threw his arms open and pulled Esme towards him in a bear hug. Then speaking mostly into her hair he added:

"And I know someone else who will be pleased."

"Oh yes, Hetty has already planned her trip in advance," Esme replied cheerfully, as Andrew planted a kiss on top of her head.

"She said she'd come and give me a tour of the city if I got in."

"Did she now?" said Andrew, raising his eyebrow.

"Just don't let her take you to the Maison Souquet!"

"Daddy!" Esme scolded playfully, rolling her eyes. Then she turned to Sienna:

"Mum?" she said, her eyes wide with hope. Sienna was gazing back at her, so overwhelmed by love it was hard to find the words.

"My beautiful girl," she said, smoothing a strand of hair away from her daughter's face.

"I thought I couldn't be any more proud of you. But I was wrong. Come here," she added, pulling Esme into her chest.

"Being back with you this past year has been the most magical time of my life. You deserve all the riches that are coming your way."

Mother and daughter embraced like that for a moment or two. Then Esme pulled back. She looked at her parents' faces, bursting with pride, and felt a sensation in the pit of her stomach she'd not had since her Mum had returned.

"But I'll feel so sad leaving you both behind," she said, her voice cracking like it used to when she'd fallen over as a little girl.

"I mean it was just me and Dad for all those years. And I've only just got Mum back. And…"

Sienna took her daughter's hand in hers and gazed into her eyes.

"This is your moment," she said gently.

"You've done so much for your father and I already, it would take a lifetime for us to ever repay you. It's time for you to go out into the world now. Let everyone see what an incredible woman Esme Drake has grown into."

"Speaking of grown ups…" Andrew said, giving his wife a wink, before turning to Esme.

"When are you going to break the Paris news to that lovely man of yours?"

"Bobby?" Esme said with a meek smile.

"He's coming down this evening actually. Oh and he's bringing his grandad. You guys should come for dinner with us. I know Bernard is dying to catch up with you."

"And me him," Andrew said warmly.

"I swear it was that kind letter he sent to Mr Bartholomew after we'd first met, which led to me finally getting my fellowship at All Souls. I must buy that man a beer."

Bernard had sent Mr Bartholmew a letter, saying how generous Andrew had been to him on Magdalen Bridge on May Day morning. Andrew had promptly written back and the pair had struck up a friendship, which had eventually led to him offering Esme his caravan in Wales to recuperate after the accident. Over the weeks that followed, Bernard's eighteen year old grandson Bobby had been instructed to take her out for regular walks on the beach with the other Bernard in his life: a lovable but languorous Saint Bernard dog named Colin. As Esme's strength grew, so did their feelings for one another. Which meant, to Freddy's utter amazement, Esme returned to Oxford with a bona fide boyfriend.

Seeing the happiness on her daughter's face, Sienna nudged Andrew, to remind him that there was more.

"Oh yes," he said, straightening himself up, adjusting his glasses so that he was fully focused.

"We've actually got a little bit of news of our own."

Esme slowly turned towards him, wondering what on earth could be next on this day of revelations.

"Yes…?" she replied hesitantly.

"Well since the curse of you know who has been lifted," he went on.

"Our fortunes have taken a turn for the better too. It turns out that your grandparents always kept faith that your mother would return one day. So they set aside a little money to be passed on by their solicitor in the event. Which means…"

"We're moving back into our house in Summertown," Sienna said, beaming at them both with delight.

"We've got the house back?" said Esme, clapping her hands to her face and looking from her Mum to her Dad in amazement.

"My goodness, there's so much wonderful news today I'm beginning to wonder if I'm dreaming!"

Andrew gave his daughter a playful pinch, before shaking his head and saying:

"Nope, definitely not dreaming. It would appear that this is officially our 'one wild and precious life'. And one that is looking brighter by the day!"

The three of them gazed happily at one another, before

continuing to lay out their picnic in a sunny haze. Esme's soul was so full of joy, she felt certain that this day would stay in her heart forever more. She imagined taking out her easel and painting it, with her family finally back together, nestled in a dreamland of green. Then gazing up to the sky with its infinite blue, she sighed. What a summer of endless blessings this had been!

---

Printed in Great Britain
by Amazon